TIME PRESENT AND TIME PAST

Deirdre Madden

TIME PRESENT AND TIME PAST

Europa
editions

Europa Editions
214 West 29th Street
New York, N.Y. 10001
www.europaeditions.com
info@europaeditions.com

Library of Congress Cataloging in Publication Data is available
ISBN 978-1-60945-207-0

Madden, Deirdre
Time Present and Time Past

Book design by Emanuele Ragnisco
www.mekkanografici.com

Cover photo © robert_s/Shutterstock

Prepress by Grafica Punto Print – Rome

Printed in the USA

For Lara Marlowe

Time present and time past
Are both perhaps present in time future,
And time future contained in time past.
—T. S. ELIOT, *Burnt Norton*

TIME PRESENT
AND TIME PAST

Where does it all begin? Perhaps here, in Baggot Street, on the first floor of one of Dublin's best restaurants, on a day in spring. It seems as good a place to start as any. Fintan is sitting at table before the ruins of a good lunch, with crumbs on the tablecloth and empty wine glasses, together with half-empty bottles of mineral water, both still and sparkling. There are two tiny coffee cups on the table, and a crumpled white linen napkin discarded on the place opposite. One might imagine that a disgruntled lover has just flounced off, but Fintan, faithful as Lassie, is not that kind of man. His lunch companion has been a business associate and the encounter has not gone well; it has been both strange and unpleasant. For now, Fintan dwells on the unpleasantness, and on the lunch itself.

He has eaten a fine sea bass, that most fashionable of fish, but, distracted by the obstinacy of the other man, he has not particularly enjoyed it. He feels irritated too, because when the waitress brought dessert menus his companion had waved them away, even though he, Fintan, was the host. They ordered espressos and the other man threw his back as though it were a shot of vodka, then said he must leave. It was a cool parting. Fintan broods on all of this and eats the chocolate almonds that came with his coffee. Instead of solving problems with the help of hospitality, as he had intended in arranging the lunch, it has further complicated and compounded the difficulties. He eats the chocolate almonds that came with the other man's coffee. It is Ireland in the spring of 2006 and failure, once an integral part of the national psyche, is an unpopular concept these days. Fintan feels the snub of the dismissed dessert menus with particular keenness.

His full name is Fintan Terence Buckley and he is forty-seven years old. He is a legal advisor at an import/export firm, and a more successful man than he feels himself to be. He has been married to Colette, who is the same age, for twenty-four years. They live in Howth and have two sons: Rob, who is studying business and economics at University College Dublin; and Niall, who is in his first year of art history and English at Trinity. They also have a daughter, Lucy, who is seven.

He finishes his coffee and settles the bill. As he goes downstairs, to his dismay he recognises two of the diners in the packed ground floor: his mother Joan and her sister Beth. He feels a further stab of dislike for the man who walked out on him, and who would have been the perfect decoy at this moment, for he could have swept past with little more than a smile and a greeting. Now he cannot avoid them. He tells himself he is being foolish. It will be good to talk to Beth. He tells himself not to get annoyed, no matter what his mother says to him. He buttons the jacket of his suit, unbuttons it, buttons it again, and then crosses to where they are sitting.

'Hello Mummy, hello Auntie Beth.' Fintan hates calling his mother 'Mummy.' It makes him feel like a little child, but she resists 'Mum' and all other alternatives. They exchange greetings, a flurry of air kisses and grey hair, soft flowery scent. His mother is formidable in fuschia; Beth is wearing a navy suit.

'This is a lovely surprise,' Beth says. Both women have menus in their hands; they have yet to order their meal. Beth urges him to join them and he replies that he has just lunched with a colleague.

'You call it work, I suppose,' his mother says. 'Isn't it well

for some. Work indeed.' Given that the lunch was most definitely to be filed under work, this irritates Fintan. He is dou-
bly irritated, because he had resolved not to let his mother
annoy him, and she has succeeded in doing so in less than a
minute. He doesn't respond but says to Beth, 'What are you
thinking of having?'

'And you'll have had a pudding, too, if I know you,' his
mother goes on, ignoring the fact that she is being ignored.

'I didn't,' Fintan says. She reaches out and jabs him in the
stomach with her index finger.

'You'll go home tonight and have another full dinner. No
wonder you're the shape you are. Look at you!' And she jabs
him again.

'Ah leave him be, Joan,' Beth pleads, 'isn't he grand? I'm
thinking of having the sea bass, Fintan.'

'It's the wrong day of the week for fish,' Joan says, turning
her attention to the menu again. 'It can't possibly be fresh.
They'll give you some old thing that's been lying in the fridge
since last Friday.'

'It sounds rather good,' Beth says. 'It comes with spinach
and new potatoes.' Fintan tells her that it is good, that he had
it himself and that it was both delicious and fresh.

'Have the lamb, Beth,' Joan says. 'That's what you want.'

*If she wants the lamb then why is she saying that she wants
the bloody sea bass?* It's a mercy Martina isn't here, Fintan
thinks, or there'd be war. A foreign waitress comes to the table,
wearing a shirt and tie and a black waistcoat. The lower half of
her body is wrapped in a long white linen apron and she is
holding a notepad.

'Are you ready to order?' Fintan puts his hand lightly on
Beth's shoulder and says, 'This lady is having the sea bass, and
might I suggest a glass of Sancerre to go with it. Mummy, you
were interested in the lamb?'

'I'll have the beef, and a glass of Brouilly, if I'm let,' she says, snapping the menu closed and holding it out. The waitress proposes mineral water and then leaves.

Because his sister is in his mind Fintan asks Beth, 'How's Martina doing these days?'

'She's very well. She was talking about you only last evening. Come and see us, we'd love that.' She asks after Colette then, asks about Lucy and the boys. Her gentle sincerity soothes Fintan after his run-in with his mother, at whom he glances as he talks to Beth. Joan is still bristling, like a cat that has been pushed out of its favourite chair. Beth throws her a few easy conversational openings, but she does not respond. She sits there, staring at her own hands, which, Fintan notices, look considerably older than the rest of her. The bright stones of her rings, rubies, an emerald, their startling colours, are disconcertingly at odds with the mottled and gnarled fingers that display them. Now Fintan feels small and mean for being angry with such an elderly woman, particularly one who happens to be his own mother. *But she started it.* Thinking this makes him feel smaller still, and meaner.

The waitress returns with the wine. He wishes them well for their meal and takes his leave.

* * *

He walks up Baggot Street, up Merrion Row, past offices and busy shops, past other restaurants full of patrons like himself, businessmen in suits. As he goes, he tries to rationalise to himself the irritations of the day. True, he has let Joan annoy him, but against that, he in his turn has annoyed her and, perversely, this makes him feel better. He reflects that, compared to his sister, he has a relatively good relationship with their mother. Had he not already been in poor humour because of his unsuccessful meeting, he might well have found the encounter tolerable. But today he feels sufficiently bothered and dispirited not to want to go back to work immediately. He sees Stephen's Green ahead of him and decides that he will go in there for a moment to clear his head.

Fintan crosses the road and enters behind the statue of Wolfe Tone. He walks along the lovely alley of lime trees and then turns towards the water. Up on the humpbacked stone bridge he looks left, to where a lone mallard is dragging a vast triangular wake across the still surface of the pond. There are more birds on the other side of the bridge, mallards and moorhens and swans. Children are feeding them bread and as Fintan watches he thinks of his own daughter Lucy. Lucy, whose conception he had resented, whose birth he had dreaded, and whom he loves (he can admit this only to himself) more than anyone else in his life. He will bring Lucy here so that she too can throw crusts to the birds. He will take her to the playground in the Green; he will point out squirrels in the trees; he will lay down memories for her to enjoy in the years ahead, like fine wines maturing in a cellar. But when he tries to visualise Lucy as an adult, as the woman who will savour these memories, he cannot do it. All he can see is a pearly mist: something like ectoplasm.

For all that, Fintan already feels happier than he was when he left the restaurant. He walks on to where the Green opens up into a series of gaudy flowerbeds and he stops to check his phone. There is a voicemail from his assistant saying that his three o'clock meeting has been cancelled, and this cheers him further. He texts Colette to ask what's for dinner. Unusually, he decides to take a somewhat free-form approach to the afternoon. He will not go back to the office just yet. He will go and have a cup of coffee, and perhaps something sweet to make up for being gypped out of his dessert. His phone chirps twice. *Roast chicken thought u had lunch out 2day?* Fintan doesn't reply but continues on to the Ranger's cottage, and this too he resolves to point out to Lucy. It will be pleasing to a child, this gingerbread house, with its exaggeratedly steep roof and elaborate edging, its tiny bright garden and boxwood hedges, absurdly pretty. He leaves the Green by the gate behind the cottage and crosses over to Harcourt Street, and goes into a cafe there.

At the counter he orders a latte and a piece of carrot cake. (Unfortunately Joan is correct: he does need to lose weight.) The waitress hands him the cake and says she will bring the coffee down to him. There are bentwood chairs and marble-topped tables in the cafe. From where he chooses to sit, Fintan can see out into the street, to the little wooden terrace where the smokers sit. He can also see a wall hung with black-and-white photographs of Dublin at the start of the twentieth century. There is the famous one of the train accident at Harcourt Street Station, the locomotive slammed right through the wall and out the other side, like a toy an angry child had broken in a rage; and there are pictures of the streets Fintan himself has recently walked, of the Green itself, but peopled here with citizens in long awkward dresses and bustles, kitted out with parasols and hats. There is pop music on the radio, one of the FM stations with chatty DJs to cheer people up, to get them through the day, to distract them with things they will immediately forget.

The waitress brings the coffee. The cake, which he now opens and starts to eat, is packaged in a small cardboard sleeve, the whole thing wrapped in cellophane. On one side are the words 'A Sweet Treat' and on the other side 'Carrot Cake.' As Fintan drinks his latte, he listens to the music and gazes absentmindedly at the words 'Carrot Cake' until all meaning drains out of them. The letters are just shapes, random and arbitrary, and have no connection to what they describe. They might as well be written not just in a foreign language but in a different alphabet, might as well say бИСКВИТ or ΤΤαντΣΟΤάνί. Fintan is aware that this kind of thing is not so unusual, that pretty well everyone has had this experience of looking at a word somewhere until the meaning detaches from the word itself, although they tend to come together again as soon as one becomes aware of it. But it isn't just words and language that are becoming strange to him, it is objects too. What had been in the cardboard sleeve now looks unspeakably bizarre to him: the moist terracotta crumbs; the coarse, bright-orange shreds laced through it; the heavy parchment-coloured cream in which is embedded a thing, a hard, dark wrinkled thing that looks like the pickled brain of an elf. And now, like the fading of a dream, Fintan gradually becomes aware of the object before him for what it is: a half-eaten piece of carrot cake with a walnut on top.

What rattles him is that this is the second time today that such a thing has happened. When he had been having lunch, at a certain point he had stopped hearing, or indeed listening to, what his companion was saying. The other man had stopped being a person with whom Fintan was communicating, and had become instead a kind of phenomenon which he was observing. It was as if the air had thinned out and the man was like something that had dropped out of the sky. Fintan had stared at his face, which was florid, at the way his bulging neck flowed over the hard edge of his shirt collar. The lilac silk tie had a luxurious sheen; he noticed the way there was a kind of white light in where it curved in the knot. Maybe it was something of the contrast between his companion's imperfect body and the expensive details of his attire that had triggered all of this. And all the time he was staring at him the man was talking, about what Fintan had no idea. He couldn't even hear him properly; it had been like watching a film with the sound turned down. Suddenly he realises that this might well be a reason why the meeting had gone so badly: he had perhaps missed some important point that the other man had made, or the man had become aware that Fintan wasn't mentally present in the way he should have been, and this had perplexed or even annoyed him. And now this strange thing in the cafe.

He tells himself to get a grip. He looks again at the photographs. There is a dislocation between the familiarity of the locations and the strangeness of what is shown: the clothes, the transport. The trams in the pictures are packed and seem too small to be taken seriously, with people hanging off the top as if they could only be riding along for a lark, rather than for necessity. Dublin at the start of the twentieth century looks cluttered and weirdly complex, with the fussy dresses of the women, with the elaborate shop fronts. Fintan suddenly realises that he finds it difficult to believe in the reality of these scenes. He can no more imagine himself on the streets alongside these people, who lived in the same city as him, than he can imagine himself as a figure on a Grecian urn. Is it because the images are in black and white that they seem irredeemably distant? But once Beth had shown him a photograph which reconciled the past and the present: an Edwardian miss with a straw hat, some long-forgotten ancestor of theirs, who bore an extraordinary resemblance to Fintan's sister Martina. And he remembers now also a remark Lucy had made once when they were trawling through a box of old family photographs at home: weddings, rainy picnics, late lamented terriers. 'When did the world become coloured?' It had taken him a moment to understand what she meant, and then he thought he had never heard such a delightful notion. He loved the idea of a monochrome world suddenly flooded with colour.

Out on the street, beyond the wooden deck, the Luas slips past, a sleek and silver tram, almost futuristic in spite of its quaintly chiming bell. Fintan finishes his coffee and cake. It's time for him to get back to the office.

Already he is thinking about dinner.

Two

B y mid-afternoon Joan and Beth have finished their lunch, and they leave the restaurant. They say goodbye to each other and Beth heads off in the direction of the National Gallery, while Joan unwittingly retraces her son's steps along Merrion Row, going towards the Green. Like Fintan, she also goes into the gardens, and sits down on a bench near the ponds, to get her bearings and decide what to do with the rest of her day.

She's glad that the lunch is over. It had been pleasant enough, but she always finds it something of an obligation, a chore even, to meet Beth. Even though they're sisters, they don't have much in common. Beth is interested in music and gardening, things which Joan has never found particularly engaging. They always talk a little bit about the family, of course, although rarely about Martina, who actually lives with Beth. And so their conversation had stayed on the most general of topics: the meal they were eating, holiday plans, the weather and so on. There's no point talking to Beth about topics that really interest Joan, such as the economy. She reads every last little article in the business pages of *The Irish Times* every day and is convinced that the good times are going to end, and sooner rather than later. Anybody should be able to see it coming, she thinks. The problem is that people don't want to know, they want to think that the money will keep flowing forever. Well, they're in for a shock.

Joan feels happier and more relaxed now that she's on her

own again. She leans back on the bench and gazes out over the water. It had been a funny coincidence seeing Fintan like that, in the restaurant. Fat as a fool he is, these days. It's bad for his health. She resolves to tell him as much the next time she sees him. She'll remind him to go and get his cholesterol checked; no, better than that, he needs one of those comprehensive medical tests that they do now in the private clinics. Have blood samples taken, get his heart checked out. That's what she'll tell him to do. She'll mention it to Colette as well and have a word with her about his diet. He eats too much; he was always a glutton. Maybe Colette can help persuade him to go to the clinic, because Fintan is like most men, he won't go near the doctor no matter what's wrong with him. If his head fell off and rolled across the floor, he'd pick it up and stick it back on, hope for the best. Fintan's own father had been exactly the same and where did it lead? To a heart attack in his prime, that's where, and Joan left on her own to finish rearing Fintan and Martina.

She sighs and shakes her head. Enough. The rest of the afternoon is hers to enjoy as she thinks fit. She doesn't come into the centre of town very often these days, so when she does, she likes to make the most of it. She'll do a little shopping and then have a cup of tea somewhere before getting the DART home. This plan pleases her and she looks forward to the next hour or so.

She leaves the Green by Fusiliers' Arch, crosses the road and walks down Grafton Street past all the buskers: past a man pretending to be a statue and another man making enormous soap bubbles that quiver and wobble; past a group playing traditional Irish music. It's quite busy in town today. There are shoppers and tourists; there are young women wearing those little sheepskin boots that look like slippers, together with short skirts and opaque tights. It's an odd look, Joan thinks. They're probably students from Trinity, for some of them have satchels over their shoulders that gape open, showing folders and books.

She goes into Brown Thomas and walks through the glittering cosmetics hall, where girls in black dresses and high heels attempt to spritz her with the latest expensive new perfume. Skinny Minnies all of them, and wearing far too much makeup, they remind Joan of Martina at the same age. It isn't a happy thought. She sweeps imperiously past them, and heads for the escalator.

Joan finds herself reflected in mirrors everywhere. She's a handsome woman, big boned, with strong features, and she takes pride in her appearance. Although she's in her seventies now she could pass for late sixties. A snappy dresser, she's looking today for a new suit for the spring, something that will take her on through to the summer. She likes classic, rather formal clothes—Basler, Jaeger, things that don't date.

As she browses through the racks she notices two women, one about her own age and one a good deal younger. It's clearly a mother and daughter out shopping together, because they look quite like each other. The mother has just come out of the changing room, in a dress with a big label hanging on the back of it, and the daughter is giving her opinion. Joan has never liked shopping with other people, certainly not for clothes, and certainly not with Martina. Very occasionally she'll go shopping with Colette, but only for things for the house. Colette helps her bring home in the car items that would be too big for her to manage on her own. But Joan knows her own mind. She either likes something or she doesn't. Beth, on the other hand, is a born ditherer. Joan suspects that she wouldn't have a clue how to dress without Martina's help; why, she even used to let Christy tell her what colours she should wear, because she couldn't make up her mind for herself.

After looking around for a while, she settles on two possible options, both of them in summer-weight wool. One is a dress and matching jacket in black-and-white houndstooth; the other a skirt suit in a soft turquoise colour. She feels that she would get more wear out of the houndstooth, but she likes the other one much more. The colour is flattering and is more suitable, she thinks, for the season that's in it. She tries both of them on, and quickly settles on the turquoise one. It's an easy decision to make.

Once she's paid for the suit and it's been presented to her in a striped carrier bag, she browses around the store a little more, and then goes out onto Grafton Street and looks in a few more shops, at shoes and scarves.

By now she's ready for some tea, and so she heads through the arcade that leads onto Dawson Street, and goes up Molesworth Street to the National Museum, the cafe of which is a favourite place of Joan's. You can almost always get a table there, even though the room is small, and it has a certain elegance with its chandelier, the chain supporting it swagged in silk. Another advantage, she thinks, as she waits for her pot of Earl Grey, is that you're almost certain to be left in peace. The risk of running into someone you know in the museum is very slight.

She sits down with the tea and waits for it to draw. There's a younger woman at a nearby table with an enormous buggy. It's quite ridiculous, the size of it: you could invade Iraq in a thing like that, Joan thinks. There's a changing bag hooked onto the handles of the buggy; and the front is all hung with toys, trinkets and little mirrors, like a pagan shrine. Joan pours her tea and savours its citrus fragrance.

An elderly man sitting on the other side of her politely asks for a salt shaker off her table, and she passes it to him with a smile. They talk to each other for a few moments before the man continues with his meal. Joan quite likes talking to strangers: fellow passengers on the bus or the DART; people walking their dogs along the seafront near where she lives, or sitting on park benches. She likes that glancing interaction, where nothing is at stake. People don't know who you are; there's no emotional baggage, no *intimacy*. Joan hates the very word, with its connotations of privacy violated, of things that shouldn't even be thought of being dragged into the open. *Intimate friends*: who in their right mind would want such a thing?

Of course she couldn't say it to anyone, they'd only take it up wrongly, but she loves being a widow. That isn't for a moment to say that she's glad her husband Terence died; it's rather that she's very happy living alone, and never having to please anyone but herself. Joan never tires of her own company.

As she drinks her tea she remembers the Trinity girls she'd seen on Grafton Street earlier. Did they know how lucky they were to be at university? Joan would have given anything to have gone to college, but her father hadn't believed in education for girls. Business, politics, economics, law, even: Joan would have loved to study any one of those subjects, and she'd have had the brains for it too, for she'd been a smart young woman. It had annoyed her beyond measure that Martina had had every opportunity to study and had made nothing of it. Terence had always said she wasn't academic, but he had doted on her and made excuses. It was just laziness, as far as Joan could see. Martina had never been interested in anything other than lipsticks and dresses, boys and going to dances. Even Fintan could have done better as far as education went. He got his law degree, he was clever and hard-working and had quite a good job now, but he didn't have the right personality, Joan thought, he had been too soft-hearted to ever end up as a judge or a barrister. Still, she has great hopes for his sons, for Rob in particular.

She and Beth had both entered the civil service after they left school. If it was good enough for their own father, the logic had run, it should have been good enough for them. They'd started at quite a lowly level, in clerking posts, and Beth, in all the years she spent there, had never made any great progress. She'd had no real interest or aptitude; it had never been anything more than a way to make a living. But Joan had been ambitious. She'd worked hard, studied at night, sat exams and moved slowly up through the grades.

What if my life had been different? she wonders now, gazing into her tea cup and staring at the leaves, as if trying to predict her own future instead of reassess the past. What if I had never married? But in those days the only way for a woman to be respected was to get a ring on her finger. Joan had always known that. She'd hated being stuck living at home, but back in the day you couldn't just move out to a place of your own. She'd used to envy the girls in the civil service who were up from the country, for even though they were only in boarding houses or sharing dingy little flats together, at least they'd had their freedom and their privacy.

Terence Buckley had been a young teacher lodging in a house two doors down from Joan's family home, and her connection with him had started in small talk when they met on the street. It's odd, but she suspects that she thought about marriage before he did, even though when it came to the point it was he who had had to persuade her. He'd been a decent man, gentle and soft spoken, so she'd known she would be fine with him. She didn't want anyone who was short-tempered like her father; she didn't want anyone who had a stronger will than her own. She hadn't been looking for trouble; she'd wanted a home that was truly hers; wanted to get away from her wretched, bickering parents. The big problem had been the marriage bar. In those days women had been obliged to give up their civil service jobs when they got married, so it hadn't been an easy decision to make. She'd thought about it for a long time before deciding to throw in her lot with Terence.

She'd been correct in her assessment of him, for he'd turned out to be a good husband and father; a steady worker who ended up a headmaster, and an excellent provider for the family. Marriage, in fairness, hadn't been so bad. It was the children that had been the real problem.

But no, she thinks immediately, stealing a glance at the monster buggy beside her, that wasn't true: it was the having of the children she had hated. To this day she can hardly bring herself to walk past the National Maternity Hospital. She regards it as she feels the citizens of Moscow must have regarded the Lubyanka during the Purge: as an imposing civic building in the centre of the city, within the walls of which truly unspeakable things were happening day and night. She hadn't had too hard a time of it with Fintan for she hadn't been sick when she was expecting him, just tired all the time, and then when he was ready to be born she didn't realise what was happening until the last gasp; she'd almost had him right outside the hospital, on the pavement of Holles Street. It was the second time around that she had really suffered.

There'd been the so-called morning sickness that had lasted all day, every day, for pretty well the whole nine months, until she thought she would surely bring up her own liver and lights, because it didn't seem possible that there could be anything else left inside her that she hadn't vomited up. She'd been pregnant over the course of a summer, an unusually close and humid summer, which had added greatly to her discomfort. Labour had lasted for three days, three days of indescribable pain and humiliation. And then the baby, when she finally brought it home, had colic. It wouldn't sleep and it whinged all the time, 'a gurney baby,' as Terence's mother up in the North had called it. She'd only realised then how easy a time of it she'd had with Fintan and even later, as a little boy. There'd never been any trouble managing him, for he'd been an obedient child, Joan thinks, tractable. But she doesn't like to remember those early days of motherhood, not even now, so many years later.

She finishes her tea and decides that she'll head for home soon. She won't need to do any cooking tonight, having had a solid lunch with Beth, just put out a few cold cuts and some bread, maybe cheese and some fruit. Everything she needs is in the house, and there's red wine too. She'll have a glass, just the one, then she'll read the paper, do the crossword and watch the news on television before having an early night.

There are worse things to be than a widow in your seventies. Sometimes Joan wonders if there's anything better.

A s promised, Colette has roasted a chicken. She has cooked small potatoes; she has steamed carrots and green beans. When Fintan goes into the kitchen their younger son, Niall, is there with his mother, preparing salads. The back of his T-shirt reads, '. . . do all the other trees laugh?' Niall is a strict vegetarian. He eats with the family but makes his own meals, an arrangement that has been in place without rancour for years now. Fintan, who is interested in all food, approaches and looks in the pottery bowls on the worktop. Niall has made a three-bean salad with a vinaigrette dressing; a green salad; quinoa with tomatoes, red onion and mint. Fintan says, 'The beans look tasty, Niall.' Niall turns to him and smiles amiably. 'Yeah, but you're not getting any, Dad.' The front of his T-shirt reads, 'If a tree falls in the forest . . .'

Lucy arrives in the kitchen, followed by Rob, her eldest brother, just as the chicken is being carried to the table. Rob is small and pale and dressed all in black which makes him look sinister, a look he might well be cultivating, Fintan thinks. The whole family is now here for dinner, and this is not an unusual event. It is something Fintan has always encouraged ever since the boys were small. He is not a strongly paternalistic man, at least he doesn't think so, but, in his fondness for seeing his family gathered around a table laden with food, he is as traditional as Bob Cratchit. Rob brings the serving dishes with the vegetables while Colette sets a stack of heated plates beside Fintan, who is now sharpening the carving knife.

Like her husband, Colette could do with losing a little weight. She is also rather a plain woman, something of which she is acutely aware, but which other people almost never remark upon because she is inordinately kind, and this kindness, suffusing her face, makes her look more attractive than many a cold beauty half her age. She is wearing a dreadful old jumper with a hole in the elbow, a green Aran knit that she bought on a holiday in Connemara when the boys were small. It looks a fright, and Colette knows this, but it is comfortable as a second skin. She hands Fintan a two-pronged fork with a folding safety guard, and he begins to carve the fowl, as Lucy digs serving spoons into the vegetables.

'This is great, Mum,' Rob says.

'It looks like a chicken in a cookery book,' Lucy says brightly, which it does, with a charred half-lemon protruding from its rear end, and its varnished breast scattered with sprigs of thyme.

When Rob was born it had been a shock to Fintan, who realised immediately he knew nothing about babies. With hindsight he saw that he had expected something fragrant and beguiling, something more like a teddy bear than the vital little animal that Rob turned out to be.

While still in his cot he had the thousand-yard stare of a hostile banker. His physical strength and his strength of will astounded Fintan. At six months the baby sucked his thumb, and Fintan discovered that he couldn't dislodge the digit from his mouth by using gentle pressure; was alarmed to realise that he couldn't do it even if he applied brute force: Rob was still able to resist him. Fintan took to calling him 'Stalin,' but Colette didn't see the joke, and made him desist. Unlike her husband she was skilful with the baby. She could hold him at her hip with one arm while engaging in some complicated domestic chore with the free hand; could sling him artfully over her shoulder and make him burp; could make him stop crying any time she wanted by cunningly distracting him with small stuffed toys. It was a relief when, around the time of Rob's first birthday, Colette said she was expecting another baby. *Yes, let's have another go at this,* Fintan had thought. *Let's get it right this time.*

It was certainly different second time around. So placid was Niall that he quickly became known as 'The Potato.' He lay in his pram smiling and cooing, gazing into space, as if he hadn't noticed that he had been born, as if he was still in some Edenic, prenatal world where everything was beautiful and good. Complete strangers stopped in the street to peer in at the beaming baby; and he grew into a blissed-out toddler who was happy to share his toys and treats with all-comers. To his dismay, Fintan wasn't completely at ease with all of this, and couldn't help finding Niall's extreme gentleness, his even temper and his Buddha-like smile slighty spooky. He found himself wondering if there could have been some kind of mix-up in the maternity ward, so that they had brought home someone else's baby. Aged five, when told to say goodbye to Joan on a family visit, Niall took her hand and said solemnly, 'Granny, I hope you will always have love and peace in your heart,' a moment that has passed into family legend and which Niall himself now finds hilarious. (Rob: 'You totally mad little hippy.') At six he made the connection between animals and meat and displayed an unexpected moral rigour about it, pushing his rashers and sausages around the plate, refusing to eat, and weeping inconsolably for the fate of the poor pig when pressed to do so; even at times displaying an uncharacteristic sharpness and sarcasm, holding up a chop on his fork: 'What did you have to kill to give me this?' The family doctor reassured them, and gave Colette diet sheets as they realised they had no choice but to accept the tiny vegetarian in their midst.

In the meantime Rob had continued to grow into a tough little alpha male, and Fintan, to his shame, found it hard to connect with either of them. He felt like Charlie Chaplin in *The Kid* when he gives Jackie Coogan a gentle boot in the arse, trying to get shot of him, trying to make out that he wasn't responsible for this little tyke. It had been a relief when Colette had indicated that the family was complete with the two boys.

Niall now looks pointedly at Fintan's heaped plate.

'Weren't you having lunch out today, Dad?'

'Yes, but I didn't have anything much, and anyway, that was ages ago. I saw Granny and Beth in the restaurant, quite by chance.'

Rob laughs ironically. 'Lucky you. And how was Granny? Sweet as ever she is?'

'Granny was fine,' Fintan says evenly, glancing meaningfully at Lucy and then back at Rob with narrowed eyes, mutely warning him. 'She sends her best, as does Beth.'

'Where did you go?'

Fintan names the restaurant.

Rob says, 'Cool,' and he laughs. 'Fair play to Granny and Beth for doing things in style.' It is a restaurant he likes: unlike his brother, who is somewhat ascetic, he is developing expensive habits and tastes. Colette names another place, which she prefers, and they fall to talking about restaurants as they eat, then about how the day has been.

They all do a double take when Niall says, 'I saw a woman on Grafton Street today with no skirt.' Lucy whoops with delight.

'What was she wearing then?' Fintan and Rob ask simultaneously, and they all laugh.

'Her knickers. And a pink sash thing over her blouse, like a beauty queen, you know? And a tiara. She was with a bunch of friends. They were all wearing sashes too, with "Tracy's Hen Night" printed on them, but they didn't have tiaras and they all had their skirts on. I know what you're thinking,' he adds, looking frankly at his brother, 'but to be honest, it wasn't a pretty sight. You were lucky you missed it.'

'But why?' asks Lucy, who is still laughing. 'Why was the woman going down Grafton Street in her knickers?'

'Because she's getting married,' Colette says. 'Eat your carrots, please.'

'But why?' Lucy asks again. 'Did you do that, Mum, before you got married? Did you walk down the street with no skirt?'

'I did nothing of the sort!'

'Perish the thought,' says Rob with feeling, and his mother flicks at him with her napkin. But they are all laughing now, Colette most of all and Lucy without really understanding why.

'I'm invited to a sleepover at Emma's house next Friday,' Lucy says, and again Fintan narrows his eyes. This time he stares hard at Colette, quizzically. She stares back unblinking. Emma is Lucy's best friend. Emma's parents are divorced and she divides her time between her mother, who also lives in Howth, and her father, who lives somewhere in the vicinity, Fintan isn't exactly sure where. Fintan dislikes Emma's mother intensely. She has a new boyfriend and a new baby with the new boyfriend. He hates Lucy spending time at the mother's house, although Colette has no problem with it. Emma is a sullen, rather difficult child, and Fintan doesn't know what Lucy sees in her.

'Emma could come here instead,' he suggests.

'That's what I said,' Colette adds.

'But it's my turn to stay with her.'

'It doesn't always have to be turn and turn about, does it? There's no rule. If she comes here,' Fintan adds, 'I'll plan a special surprise for the Saturday.'

'Will you, Daddy? Something nice?' Lucy asks coquettishly.

'Something horrible,' Rob says. 'A cold bath and turnip sandwiches.' She giggles with delight at this. 'Raw turnip. That would be a surprise, wouldn't it?'

Fintan is about to say, 'Something amazing,' and then he thinks better of it, because he has no idea what the treat might be. He remembers the children with the mallards on the Green that afternoon, but wonders now how he had ever thought that such a blasé and frankly spoiled child of the early twenty-first century as Lucy might be charmed by such a modest outing. She habitually visits the seals down in Howth harbour, the seals that are such a fixture they are drawn on the tourist map, emerging from the waves like sea monsters or mermaids on a medieval map.

'A surprise,' he says again, to buy time to think of something. 'If I told you what it was then it wouldn't be a surprise any more, would it?' Lucy accepts the logic of this.

Talking to Lucy reminds him of his chain of thought in the Green and in the cafe, of her remark about the photographs.

'Niall,' he asks, 'do you know when colour photography was invented?'

'The early twentieth century.'

'As early as that? Are you sure?'

'Pretty sure. I don't know the exact date though.'

Fintan says, 'I thought it was later, maybe the twenties or thirties,' but Niall insists it was earlier.

'Why do you want to know, Dad?'

'I was just wondering.'

'Painting's more my thing than photography,' Niall says.

There are yoghurts and fruit for dessert. Rob makes a pot of tea for everyone and Lucy sets out the cups. Fintan wants biscuits. 'I didn't have dessert after lunch.' This is true, although somewhat disingenuous, and Rob says, 'But I bet you had a muffin in the middle of the afternoon, didn't you, Dad?' which is getting dangerously close to the fact of the carrot cake. And then at the very end of the meal, just as they are about to rise from the table, Fintan suddenly says, 'Stop.'

They all look at him.

'Could everyone just stay where they are for a moment? Don't say anything, just sit there.'

Bemused, they look at each other, but do as requested. For a short time they sit in silence, like worshipping Quakers waiting for the Spirit to move through the room. The kitchen clock ticks. Fintan looks at them all earnestly. Then he simply says, 'Thank you,' and stands up.

They begin to move plates, to tidy things away. Niall and Rob clear the table and fill the dishwasher with speed and efficiency, a routine that astonishes visitors to the house who observe their domesticity. Colette, an only daughter who was much put upon for household chores, has trained up her sons ruthlessly from an early age. Lucy insists upon putting in the powder and pressing the button to turn on the machine, and she is indulged in this, as in many things. The remains of the chicken are still on the worktop, its ravaged little carcass reminding Fintan of Christmas night; and he recognises the familiar feelings of being sated and melancholy that he experiences every year late on the twenty-fifth of December, the sense of the feast being over. Fintan loves Christmas.

He takes Lucy upstairs to prepare her for bed and to read her a story. Niall goes off to finish an essay. In the sitting room, Colette turns on the television and flops down on the sofa to watch it. Rob puts on his jacket and leaves the house to meet a friend. The dishwasher churns. The evening passes.

FOUR

C olette can't sleep. It is four in the morning, a difficult hour for humanity. It is a time when one's conscious defences are down, when one is psychically most vulnerable, prey to brooding and regrets, to dark thoughts. But Colette has no darkness in her soul, no demons. She is brooding, yes, but about nothing more sinister than the lasagne she left out of the freezer the night before. She realises now that it is too big. Rob will not be home for dinner, it has to feed only herself, Fintan and Lucy. She should have left out the fish pie instead. Beside her, Fintan is sleeping deeply. In her wakefulness she tries not to fidget and disturb him. Eventually she slides out from under the duvet, takes her dressing-gown from the hook behind the door and creeps down to the kitchen.

She considers a cup of camomile tea, and then makes the hot chocolate that she really wants. The lasagne is thawing on the worktop. It looks singularly unappetising at the moment, both icy and clammy, and it is very big indeed. Fintan will be delighted. He will have second helpings.

Colette puts out the kitchen light and takes her hot chocolate through to the sitting room. She pulls back the curtains so that there is enough light coming in from the street for her to see by; she does not need to switch on a lamp. The eerie streetlight and the green plants on the windowsill make her feel as if she is a fish in an aquarium. The chocolate is comforting, both drinking it and nursing the mug carefully against her body: she can feel the heat through her nightdress and dressing-gown.

Whatever about tomorrow's lasagne, last night's dinner was a great success, she thinks. The chicken had turned out particularly well, and even though it had only been an ordinary week night meal it had been a happy and cheerful event. Fintan had been brooding when he arrived back at the house, not quite glum, but in an odd frame of mind. Even at the end of the meal, it had to be said, asking them to sit there for a moment, what was all that about? But he'd certainly been in a better mood at the end of dinner than he had been at the start, and there was nothing new in that. Colette knows that sitting around the table with his family is what Fintan likes best in life. He is contented and relaxed then as he is at no other time. They have solved many a problem, thrashed out many a family difficulty at the end of a meal, over the last fragment of a shepherd's pie, its edges scalloped by the marks of the serving spoon; over crusts and crumpled napkins; over apple tarts that have had great wedges taken out of them.

She chuckles to herself to think of the talk of the hen party. She sees them frequently in town: little groups of women, all of them wearing pink stetsons, or all wearing angel wings; even once, mystifyingly, all dressed as bees. Colette hadn't had a hen party, not even a sedate one, and she had hated her own wedding day, had thought she looked fat and ridiculous in her big white dress. It had been like some kind of bizarre ordeal she had to go through to get Fintan. An only daughter, her mother hadn't allowed her to have the tiny private ceremony she had wanted. But Fintan had loved their wedding. He had laughed and wept and eaten and drunk and sang and danced and wept again; would even yet, in his cups, insist that there had never been a day like it.

Instead of thinking about her wedding day, Colette far prefers to dwell on the time when she had first known Fintan, when they were both students. She'd been studying modern languages (French, Spanish) for no better reason than that she had an aptitude for them, and her parents had been determined that she go to university and study *something*. He was her best friend's boyfriend's best friend, and, to begin with, they found themselves in each other's company by default, but friendship and fondness soon developed. They began to meet together on their own account. His considerable brilliance was tempered by a slight gormlessness, and while this was an unusual combination she found it both reassuring and appealing.

At that time she was still living with her parents and her brothers on one of those long, long suburban roads of identical houses, all stuck together, with little front gardens. The houses were called things like Sorrento or St. Judes; it was the quintessence of suburbia. It had seemed to her when she was a teenager as if it was expressly designed as a place to be bored in: a long bus ride from the city centre, far from the shops and the sea, far from anything that might be appealing; a wilderness of pebbledash, with Jack Russell terriers barking in the night.

Fintan was a cut above all this, with his Sandycove childhood, the good school he'd attended, and his expectation of a career in law. He had a certain social sophistication that he took for granted, but he was generous and kind, with a willingness to share his world with her. He wasn't remotely bothered by her more modest background, and in any case, their relationship was never predicated on their families. His father, of whom he appeared to have been very fond, had died when Fintan was in his last year at school. He spoke little about his mother, displaying when he did what Colette realised to be, when she herself finally met Joan, admirable restraint. One day in the street they heard someone calling, 'Martina! Martina!' and Fintan had remarked, 'That's my sister's name.' Colette finds it oddly moving to remember that, now that Martina is such an important and beloved presence in her life.

He had been slightly taken aback by the limits of her experience, of how little she had known of the city, indeed of life itself, up until then. She had never had a hot port! She had never eaten an oyster! He took her to places in the city that were unfamiliar to her, to dim snugs in pubs on rainy afternoons where they sat talking for hours, and to noisy coffee houses. They went to Wicklow on the bus and they took walks in autumn along the banks of the Grand Canal. (Perhaps they also went there in other seasons, but Colette can now recall only coloured leaves heaped along the banks above the black water.) One Sunday afternoon they went to Howth and she realised that a particularly special honour was being accorded to her, that this was somewhere that Fintan wouldn't have shared with just anyone. With hindsight she couldn't help wondering if part of its appeal was that it was on the coast but right on the far side of the bay, a long way away from where Joan lived. Colette loved it from the first, this little hilly village with its steep and winding streets, its extraordinary views out to sea. They walked along the harbour and peered down onto the oily decks of trawlers, as seabirds cried overhead. 'I'd like to live here,' Fintan had remarked on that first day. 'That would be nice,' Colette replied. She didn't think to say, 'Me too,' because it was so far beyond her aspirations, with or without Fintan.

And now the circle has closed, here she is, living with Fintan and their three children in Howth all these years later and, even though it is her own life, to think about it, to *really* think about it, astonishes her. She looks around the dim room where their possessions loom: the table she bought in an auction; the lamp that was a wedding present and which she never much liked but which has become a part of home so that she would be vexed if it was broken; Lucy's books on the table and Rob's shoes in the corner, even though she had told him to put them away in the hall cupboard before he went to bed. She has never taken taken her life for granted, and she loves her home, is grateful for it.

When she was leaving the house this morning to buy the chicken she had noticed, as she sometimes does, the sound that the front door makes. It is a sort of sigh that becomes a sharp creak as she pulls the door over, and then it closes silently, but for a click as the lock engages. After that, she has to get hold of the metal boss in the middle of the door and pull it hard towards her to properly align the second lock, the bottom one, so that it will engage when she uses the mortise key. The metal bar is audible as it slides into the jamb. All of this happens quickly as a rule—sigh—creak—click—and she doesn't pay it any special heed. But she had noticed it this morning. Although she is not particularly religious, at that moment when she locks the door she is always mindful of a thought caught somewhere between a prayer and a simple wish, that the place will be safe until she returns. As she walked away today she had thought of the empty house, of it sitting there deserted and silent, intact and sealed like a snow globe, a little closed world onto itself. Not that it was perfect, far from it: there were always things to be done—the perfection for her was that it was home.

But it was fragile too, and could be destroyed, as a snow globe can be broken, reduced in an instant to fragments of glass and the gimcrack contents that had been magnified and made magical by the water. Their lives could be overtaken by calamity; the dark act of some blank force could bring it all to an end tomorrow.

'I want to take you to meet my auntie and uncle.' He'd said it artlessly, as a child might, and even Colette, herself quite art-less and up until now more than happy with some exceptionally low-key, low maintenance dates—those noisy cafes, those walks by the canal—even Colette had demurred at this. But Fintan had coaxed her into it, albeit with nothing more original or enticing than, 'They're really nice,' and, 'I know you, you'll like them.'

Fintan's auntie and uncle lived in Drumcondra, in a slightly dingy street of red-brick houses made lovely by the cherry trees that lined it, and that happened to be in full bloom on the day of the visit. Remembering this on the sofa Colette realises that it must have been at exactly this time of year, for the cherry trees are all out now; and she remembers how the door had been opened by Christy, a little gnome of a man, and how the force of his sudden and sincere delight had blown away her shyness.

'Fintan! And . . . Colette! Colette! You're very welcome. Come in! Come in! Beth, come and see who's here.'

It was the strangest house she had ever seen. It was the house in which, Christy told her, he had grown up, and his father before him. Little or nothing had been done to change it over the years, so that it was remarkably old-fashioned. It was all wainscoting and dark-green paint, hooked rugs and framed tapestries. There was a stuffed fish in fake weed, with the name of the lake where it had been caught painted in gold letters on the glass case. There was a black piano, and an old-fashioned gramophone with a great golden horn. Even though it was spring it was a cold day, and there had been a fire burning in the grate, and on the table there was a huge vase full of daffodils that blasted the room with their yellow energy; that lit the place up more than any lamp could ever have done. It had been like going back in time, like stumbling into the pages of a story book, so that, Colette thought, if the cat on the hearth—and there was always a cat, even back then—had sat up and spoken to her, she thought that she would hardly have been surprised.

'Here's my lovely girl,' Christy said, as he introduced Beth, 'here's my sweetheart.' For that had been another strange thing about the day, strange but beguiling, as the house itself was:

the affection between them, the way they looked at each other like newlyweds, even though they were old. (Old! Colette thinks now. Why, they could only have been in their fifties.) But then again, they had only been married for a couple of years at that time, something Fintan told her on the way home afterwards, which surprised her greatly.

There had been music playing in the house that day, Beethoven and Mozart, always music, Christy's great love. He told her that he would have liked to have been a musician, but as an only child in a family of modest means, it had been more important for him to find a more solid job, and he had become a music teacher.

She wonders now why she doesn't think back consciously to that day more often, for the charge of happiness it gives her. It had made her feel closer to Fintan at the time, or rather, it had made her want to be closer to him, to remain in his life. Although already somewhat besotted with him, she found he rose considerably in her estimation after she had met Christy and Beth. To have such family enhanced him in her eyes; she wondered at the luminous hinterland of his life and what she might find there, if this was his auntie and uncle. But when she had tried to intimate as much to him, he had only said drily, 'Wait till you meet my mum.'

A lifetime ago all that had been, nigh on thirty years, and it had ended so sadly. She looks around the room again. All this will end too. It is changing all the time, although she doesn't much like to think about it. Soon the boys will be gone, would have left home already were it not for the high rents in the city. Rob in particular is keen to go, and Fintan, she suspects, is keen to see him gone. Niall feels guilty about the comfort in which he lives and that too grates on Fintan; on Colette too at times, if the truth is to be told. Maybe her own good intentions have backfired here, for when they were small she would always say to them, 'Aren't we lucky to live in such a nice place? Beside the sea, with the boats and the harbour, in such a house?' Had this been the cause of Niall's highly developed social conscience, which she found admirable and irritating in equal measure? She can see that Rob aspires to something more, that he fully approves of the moneyed climate which is contemporary Ireland, and which even Colette and Fintan feel slightly uneasy about, let alone Niall. Rob wants more material things, much more than they have given him, whereas Niall wants less, and wants to share what he does have with others.

Colette sighs and rolls over on the sofa. And what about Lucy? What about this sleepover that's supposed to happen soon and that Fintan's not keen on? How can that be squared so as to keep everyone happy? And then she's back where she started, thinking again about the lasagne. Would she be able to stretch it over two days if she made a really big salad? She decides to go into the kitchen and have a look at it, and is alarmed to find when she goes into the hall that the kitchen door is ajar and the light is on, even though she distinctly remembers turning it off, and she hasn't heard anyone coming downstairs. Gingerly she opens the door.

Lucy and her little friend Emma are sitting at the kitchen table, with the empty lasagne dish between them. Emma is putting the last forkful in her mouth as Colette comes into the room, and Lucy says to her coldly, 'It wasn't very nice, Mum.' At that, something brushes against Colette's cheek, gentle, tickling, but there is nothing there. 'You're not a very good cook, are you?' Again there's that distracting feeling of something soft against her face. She puts her hand up to brush away whatever it is. 'What are you doing here?' she says. 'I can't believe you ate the whole thing,' and for the third time, something touches her cheek. She shakes her head in irritation, and opens her eyes wide to find Fintan leaning over her, smiling.

He is holding the cord of her own dressing-gown and dangling the tassel on the end of it softly against her face to waken her. This is how they used to wake the children when they were babies, gently, so as not to startle them. The empty chocolate mug is still in her hand.

'I woke up and you weren't there,' he says, still smiling. 'Come back upstairs while the bed's still warm.'

W hen she opens the door to Fintan, Martina is wearing a cream jumper with fine grey horizontal lines, well-cut grey trousers and flat velvet pumps. He registers the general elegance of all of this, but not the detail. Unlike his own dear wife, Martina does not dress down, even when she is merely sitting at home for the evening. Not for her the worn tracksuit bottoms and holey jumper beloved of Colette. She greets him and remarks upon the weather as she leads him up the hall. Her voice has a slightly English inflection from her years in London. She is a beautiful woman, remarkably so. Even now, in her forties, people might turn to look at her in the street.

There is a fire lit in the sitting room and Beth is sitting beside it, with a tartan rug over her shoulders and a cat asleep on her lap.

'Look at her,' Martina says, as Fintan bends down to kiss his aunt. 'Isn't she like a sweet old lady out of central casting? I'm just about to spoil things and pour her a whiskey. What can I get you?'

Fintan would love to join Beth but he is driving and settles for a cup of tea, which Martina goes off to prepare. There is music playing softly in the background, a Mozart concert being broadcast on the radio. The house has changed over the years and particularly since Martina has come to live in it. There are muslin curtains on the windows where once there were dusty nets, and the gloomy green foliage, the ivies and the

Swiss cheese plants, have been replaced with potted orchids and fresh cut flowers. She has made it fresher, less dingy, but it remains a strange place, quite unlike any other house that Fintan knows of. The wind-up gramophone is still there: Beth always lets Lucy select and play a record when she comes to visit. The vases with the pink lustres, the odd woolly pictures, the hooked rugs and the big mirror, all these remain. There is still that same air of the past that Fintan remembers from his first visits here, of the quality of time itself seeming different in these rooms.

'So how was the sea bass the other day?' he says, and she laughs.

'The sea bass was grand, and I was very grateful to you for it, Fintan. If you hadn't come along when you did and backed me up, Joan would have bullied me into having something else, of that I'm quite sure. Martina was a bit cross when I told her what had happened. She's always saying I should stand up for myself, but Joan's been making me do what she wants for seventy years now, so I suppose things are hardly going to change at this late stage.' They both laugh.

'You look well, Beth.'

'I'm well looked after.' He means what he says. She looks better than she had done the other day in the restaurant. The soft light of the fire and of the lamps are kinder to her than the glare of daylight had been. She strokes the cat's head and they chat about the restaurant, about Joan and the family in general until Martina returns.

She is carrying a tray with tea and biscuits for herself and Fintan, and a cut-glass tumbler for her aunt. From the bottles on the sideboard—several types of whiskey; sherry, both sweet and dry; vodka and gin—Martina makes her choice.

'I'm going to give you some of the good stuff,' she says. When he sees the label Fintan particularly regrets that he is driving and cannot join Beth. It is a twenty-year aged whiskey, and as Martina pours it out there is the surge of a complex fragrance, tobacco and turf, a very adult smell. 'Say when.' Beth lets Martina pour her a surprisingly large measure.

'Don't tell your mummy,' she says mischievously. The whiskey is a fabulous topaz colour in the light of the fire. It has the fire of a cut jewel, the limpidity of a peaty river in the mountains as it pours over stones. Martina serves Fintan his tea, they raise their cups and glass in a toast.

'*Sláinte*,' Beth says. She takes a sip and then she closes her eyes, lies back in her chair. 'Oh, I needed that,' she says softly. Then she opens her eyes and looks sideways at Fintan. 'It helps me to sleep.'

'I bet it does,' Martina says ironically.

'It was Christy introduced me to whiskey. He was a great man for it, not that he was a heavy drinker, as you well know, but he had a great fondness for whiskey. He knew all about it; he knew how it was made. He had a grandfather worked in the distillery in Midleton and so there was always a tradition of it in the family. He had a good palate, Christy, so he was able to teach me how to tell all the different flavours and aromas there were, and he showed me the difference there was between an ordinary whiskey and one that was something special. Single malts, whiskeys that had been aged. Ah he was a great man. He taught me all kinds of things.'

Fintan looks over at Martina, expecting his glance to be acknowledged; but she is watching Beth, listening to her and smiling indulgently, as though Beth were her child rather than her aunt. The light of the fire is kind to her too. Martina is sitting holding a tea cup cradled on her lap and he notes how her looks are more striking in mundane moments such as this, when she is simply sitting by the fire, than on more formal occasions.

Martina is a great beauty, in a way that is most rare. It is more than regular features and good bones, although those attributes are certainly there: the huge clear eyes, the heart-shaped face. There's something mysterious to it. A couple of nights earlier Fintan had read *The Snow Queen* to Lucy as a bedtime story, and had found himself thinking of his sister. Not of course that she is a wicked person, but there can be something unsettling and cool about her, particularly towards men. He knows it is unfair, but he cannot help comparing her to Colette, whose kindness and guilelessness are written on her face. But you could spend a lifetime looking at Martina and wondering who she was. Her beauty suggests much more than what she is: a woman who lives with her aunt and who owns a clothes shop. There is a weight, a melancholy and mystery to her that is part of what makes her so fascinating, to both men and women; and yet it is combined with a good heart, a kindness equal to Colette's, and a jolly sense of humour, attributes that are often not immediately evident.

Martina is talking to Fintan now; she asks after all the family, what they are doing these days, how they are keeping, and she sends her love to them.

'Be sure to tell Colette,' she adds, 'that I took delivery the other day of some jackets that are just perfect for her. Tell her I'll set a few aside in her size, in different colours, and if she drops over to the shop she can see what she thinks.'

Fintan promises to pass on the message.

'Oh, and before I forget,' Martina says suddenly, 'I'll find that photograph for you.' When he had phoned in advance to say that he would visit them, as Beth had suggested, he had asked if he might see a particular old family photo that he had recently remembered. Martina gets up and fetches a small cardboard box from the sideboard.

'I left this out, but I haven't had time to go through it yet.'

She tips the box out onto the rug before the fire, spilling out a jumbled heap of all kinds of pictures: colour, black and white, sepia; snapshots and studio photographs. There are fuzzy shots from long-ago family holidays and birthdays; there is Joan looking stern and lantern-jawed at her own wedding; and a picture of Fintan himself at his First Communion, with hands neatly joined and a ribbon rosette in his jacket, but without a full complement of teeth. They laugh and talk over these until suddenly Fintan says, 'Here it is. This is the one I wanted.'

He pulls from the pile a postcard-sized sepia photograph which is pasted onto a heavy cardboard mount, a studio portrait of a young woman from the early years of the twentieth century or the end of the nineteenth. She is seated in a low armchair and is wearing a muslin summer dress, with a broadbrimmed straw hat lying on her lap. Her pose is unusually languid for the time: Fintan has seen many other photographs from that period of anxious women standing bolt upright and clutching at the backs of chairs, ill at ease and frumpy. But this woman is completely relaxed and is smiling at the camera in a way that is both beguiling and slightly unnerving. She is clearly fully conscious of her own extraordinary beauty and the power that gives her. But what gives Fintan pause is that she looks exactly like Martina, so much so that one might almost persuade oneself that it actually *is* Martina, tricked out in the clothes and accoutrements of another era. There is the same full mouth, the same huge eyes and abundant hair, the same strange smile in which there is a kind of knowledge and complexity, a sort of power. Even Martina herself, when Fintan hands the photograph back to her, admits that the resemblance they bear to each other is quite uncanny.

'And yet the sad thing is, I don't think we have any idea who she is,' Martina says as she turns the photograph over and glances at the back of it, hoping for some information there. 'Any idea?' She passes it to Beth, who narrows her eyes and peers at the image.

'Well it's my side of the family, that's for sure,' she says, 'not your daddy's, because I remember seeing this photograph in the house when I was young. It might be a sister of one of your grandparents.'

'So what would that make her to us?' Martina asks, frowning and taking the photograph back again. 'A great-aunt?'

'I suppose so.'

'Your great-grandfather,' Beth goes on, 'was a greengrocer in Rathmines.'

'Was he, indeed?' Fintan says, surprised. 'I never knew that.'

'Strange that Mummy never told us,' Martina says, 'given how proud she is of my commercial ventures.'

'Ah now Martina,' Beth pleads gently, 'you know she doesn't mean the half of it.'

Martina doesn't reply, but throws her brother a knowing look which he understands only too well, then she looks back at her other self, her beautiful ancestor. 'I hope you gave them all a good run for their money, girl.' She places the photograph on the sofa beside Fintan, and sifts again through the heap of pictures on the floor, then gives a little whoop of laughter as she pulls another one out and shows it to him.

'Do you remember this?'

It is a black-and-white photograph but Fintan doesn't laugh when he sees it, for he is too moved, and for a moment is capable of neither speech nor laughter. It is a picture of such charm as to appeal to anyone, even someone unacquainted with any of the people in the photograph. It shows a farmyard with stables. The top of one of the half-doors is open, and a horse is looking out. There is a group of people gathered around: an elderly woman, and three small children, a girl and two boys. The girl is Martina and one of the boys is Fintan. Everyone in the picture is laughing, laughing wholeheartedly. Even the horse, with its upper lip drawn back, appears to snicker.

'Granny Buckley, my God!' Fintan says eventually. 'And

Edward, he was everything to me, he was my hero when I was a kid. And me, look at the state of me!' Fintan in the photograph is a little fat buck-toothed boy with droopy socks and clumpy black shoes, bare knees and a shapeless jumper Martina's hair spouts from the side of her head in two uneven bunches, each tied with abundant ribbons and she is wearing a pale dress.

'I remember that frock, I remember arguing with Joan when she bought it, it was white with blue flowers and she wanted me to get the one with pink flowers. It was one of the rare times when I was a child when I got my own way with her.'

This surprises Fintan. His memory tells him that Martina got the better of Joan in pretty well all of their many disagreements. He has a clear memory of Martina as an adorable-looking child. At no stage in her life had she gone through a gawky or awkward phase. Thinking of her now, Fintan considers that she had been like one of those seemingly cute animals with thick fur and big round eyes—some kind of lemur, perhaps—that have razor-sharp claws concealed in their little paws, and that would slash your flesh if provoked. Martina's tiny frame had held an enormous will, and she battled against her mother in a way that had surprised Fintan. He hadn't realised that there was any option except to go to Scouts or serve Mass or go to swimming lessons or any of the other things which he didn't much care for but which his mother presented to him as an obligation. It had been a revelation when Martina flatly refused to recite a poem at the school concert, or to attend Irish dancing classes or piano lessons. There had been real battles between Joan and Martina over such things, which Fintan had observed, awestruck and slightly frightened. It had been like watching a little squaddie defy the commander in chief. It was somehow against the natural order of things and it had unsettled and disturbed him to hear Martina's tantrums, even as, deep down, he had silently egged her on.

'What colour were the stable doors? I can't remember; can you? It's a pity it's in black and white rather than colour.'

'Given how long ago it feels, it's a wonder it isn't in sepia. When exactly would this have been taken?'

Fintan stares at the photograph as he says, 'Do you know, I think that this could have been the last summer that we went up there. I'm going on the ages we look to be.'

'Do you remember arguments about it when we stopped going?'

'Vaguely. I don't think it was so much Mummy and Daddy quarrelling about it; I suspect it was more complicated and strategic than that. I think it was Granny putting pressure on Daddy. It was her wanting us to keep going back in spite of the Troubles, and him then trying to coax Mummy, and her having none of it. I suppose she had a point,' Fintan says, but Martina disagrees.

'Oh come on, Fintan, the Troubles were only an excuse. She always hated us going up there. There was no love lost between her and Granny Buckley. Can you remember Joan ever going up, even once?'

And Fintan has to admit that he can't. In all his memories of being delivered or collected when he went to stay, or on the day-trips they would make at other times of the year—in the autumn to collect apples, or at Halloween, and always before Christmas to collect a turkey—it was their father that he remembers being with them. And he recalls how there was something slightly different about him when he was back in the house where he had grown up. Fintan can see him standing on the flags of the kitchen that was dark as a cave, can see him drinking tea, talking and laughing with his mother, Fintan's Granny Buckley. But when he tries to think of his own mother there, he can't. His imagination fails at the idea of Joan sitting in that room, in the collapsed armchair beside the stove, with its hand-crocheted cushion made from scraps of coloured wool, even though it was the most comfortable chair he has ever come across; nor can he see her at the long kitchen table, whether bare or with an oilcloth on it.

'She always used to nag us before we went, "Don't be touching the farm animals because they're very dirty and if you do happen to touch them be sure to wash your hands as soon as you can afterwards." And then she used to nag us when we got back, because we might have picked up a bit of an accent.'

'Picked it up? I worked hard at mine,' Fintan says. 'I loved the way they spoke up there; I used to imitate Edward. I used to practice under my breath and repeat the things he said.'

'I came home one year and announced that I wanted to keep chickens,' Martina says, starting to laugh. 'I only did it for badness, I think, but I kept on and on about it, it really wound Joan up. I used to tell the neighbours. I used to hang over their gates and say, "We're going to get ten hens. Five black ones and five red ones, and a rooster. They're going to live in the garden and they're arriving next week." Joan was mortified. I drove her wild.'

'There was real bad feeling though, when we stopped going up there to stay.' He stares again at the photograph. 'Can I keep this?'

'Absolutely not,' Martina replies. 'But you can borrow it, so long as you keep it safe. Take her ladyship with you too, if you like, but I want her back as well.' She hands him the horse photograph, together with the picture of the young woman in the muslin dress, then glances over at Beth, who has finished her whiskey, but who has also drifted off to sleep. 'This is a pity; I'll have to waken her in a while for her to go to bed.'

She stands up and walks over to her aunt's chair, where she observes Beth in silence for some moments, with that strange gaze that Fintan recognises, and he understands the emotions Martina is feeling. It is a look of love which is not uncomplicated; which is loving, solicitious, and fearful, and which

Fintan realises probably plays on his own face, even now, when he watches Lucy sleep. It strikes him, not for the first time, how unexpected it was that Martina and Beth should end up living together. Even though they had always got on well, that was something he—indeed no one—could ever have foreseen, and he thinks of the quick terrible moves in life that brought this situation about. It has worked out well, he thinks. Whatever about Beth, he had always foreseen another life for Martina as she no doubt had for herself. As one got older, so much of life became damage limitation. He is glad they have each other. He stands and takes his leave. Martina sees him to the door and kisses him.

'Say goodnight to Beth for me.'

'I will. And don't forget to tell Colette to call over to the shop to look at the jackets. If she doesn't like them or doesn't need one, then no problem, but I'd be delighted to see her anyway.'

'She always needs new clothes,' Fintan says, with more truth than loyalty.

Six

Fintan is sitting at his desk in work. His office is on the top floor of a block near the river, and he can see all the cranes on the skyline. There are the names of construction companies fixed to them, and they turn slowly. Fintan feels ill. No, he thinks, not ill, for that would imply a simple cause and a simple cure: a tension headache and paracetamol; a stomach upset from something he had eaten. He is not sick, but a phrase turns in his mind and he cannot deny it, nor understand why it should be the truth, but there is no getting away from it: *There's something wrong with me.* He feels uneasy and anxious, yes, he is in the grip of a deep anxiety and has been so for some time now. He cannot identify what is causing it and he doesn't know how to cure it. He has a pain in the pit of his stomach that he knows comes from no physical cause, and he feels a kind of free-floating guilt about everything and nothing.

The economy appears to be roaring ahead, and although some people are now warning that a crash is inevitable, Fintan happens not to believe this. He is not against the boom—far from it, how could he be, given who he is? But when he stops to think about it, as he does now, gazing at the cranes, it adds to his anxiety rather than calms it. Many of the worst aspects of it do not touch him. He is aware of the pressure people are under and how this manifests itself in aggression when they are driving, in the abrupt service in cafes, the long commutes, the kids dumped in crèches at the crack of dawn, the lousy ready meals warmed up and eaten in front of the TV, with a glass of cheap wine to anaesthetise the effort of the whole thing: Fintan can see that this is the life so many people around him are living, and he knows how lucky he is to be escaping it.

For all that, he feels dizzy with unease. Yes, there is something wrong with him. Sometimes he feels like he has been caught in machinery; that his cuff has got trapped and he has been pulled in, so that now he is being minced and squeezed between rollers, between bright metal cylinders. He looks at the white-faced clock on the wall with its black hands. The fine red second hand sweeps around and around, he watches it with a kind of fascinated horror. Time racing on, racing like a palpitating heart, so that he feels his life will be over before he has had a chance to live it, certainly before he has had a chance to understand it. Sometimes he feels he can almost hear time rushing past him; it is like a kind of unholy wind. He wakes, he works, he sleeps, and then another day is gone and then another week.

He thinks of how, after dinner the other night, he had asked his whole family to sit quietly for a moment before they dispersed. When it happened he could hardly have said why he wanted it; it had been a spontaneous request. Now he thinks that maybe it had had something to do with the idea of stopping time, of working against just this rush of life that he finds so disturbing. He had wanted to keep the moment, to preserve it, and even by the strangeness of his request to make of it something that they might all remember.

And what had that moment been? That they were all together, yes, but also the particular atmosphere of that moment: the way the sun was shining in on the ruins of the chicken, its breastbone picked clean, the teapot, the empty cups, the faces of his family. He wanted to preserve it as other moments had in the past naturally preserved themselves for him. Some of these moments were naturally memorable—he and Colette cutting their cake on their wedding day, the burial of his father—but others were quite trivial; mundane incidents from family life which he remembered for some reason with an unnatural precision and clarity. He thought of Rob and Niall doing their homework on a wet day when they were still in national school; of a particular morning when Lucy woke up with her toy giraffe beside her and smiled at him.

Yes, his family had registered the oddness of his request over the dinner table, but what had happened when he went to visit Beth and Martina had been stranger still, even though he was certain that they had noticed nothing.

He has always found that house where they live to be rather a weird place, in spite of his fondness for it. It has a psychic force, which is not negative or bad: on the contrary. He used to think that maybe it was just the unusual way in which it was furnished, so particularly old-fashioned, that made one feel that one had entered a different reality. But he has been going there for years and nothing like this has ever happened before.

It had begun when Beth had taken her first sip of the whiskey, closed her eyes, leant back in her chair and said, 'Oh, I needed that.' That is, she spoke twice. Or rather, she didn't. She said the first phrase once, but Fintan heard it twice. She said those four words in her normal voice, which was the voice of an elderly woman; a light weak voice, like a poor sound recording. But then Fintan heard the words again, even though she did not speak. It was the voice of a much younger woman, the voice Beth must once have had, and there was a different inflection, full of passion and frank desire. 'Oh, I needed that.' And then Beth had opened her eyes, looked sideways at Fintan and said in her usual tone, 'It helps me to sleep.' 'I bet it does,' Martina had replied. She poured the tea and Fintan tried to put what had happened from his mind. Beth talked then about how she liked whiskey and how her husband had introduced her to it, ending with the remark, 'He taught me all kinds of things.' And then it happened again: the two voices, the possible double meaning and the tone so loaded that Fintan didn't know where to look. It was like an echo, an auditory hallucination. He didn't know what to make of it, and it was clearly just something to do with him for again Martina did not react or comment in any way.

And if people who are close to him are becoming strange, he is also beginning to see strangers in an intimate and overly familiar way. He had passed a female Garda in the street that morning, a small woman who had turned her head just as Fintan drew level with her, turned her bright young face towards him. Immediately he saw her no longer as she was, standing on a street corner in her functional dark uniform with its peaked cap; but sitting beside an open fire wearing the kind of cheap pyjamas they sell in Dunnes, with a motif of stars on them and her long dark hair fanned over her shoulders. He was past her by then, and didn't dare to look back.

And then on the DART, going home the previous evening, he had sat opposite a young man with carroty hair cropped short, who was crouched so low over his phone as he texted that all Fintan could see was the crown of his head and the rims of his ears. It had been a disturbing sight; it had dehumanised him to Fintan, who imagined the boy as a body on an operating table, as a corpse, even, until the boy had looked up to show his living face, his freckles and clear blue eyes.

Just remembering all of this makes Fintan feel panicky. To break the mood he gets up from his desk and crosses over to the window, is standing looking at the city skyline and thinking about all of this when suddenly there is a knock on the door of his office, and his colleague Imelda comes in without waiting for a response.

'Have you signed those contracts, Fintan?'

He stares at her. She is wearing a chalk-stripe suit, a skirt and jacket. Her blouse is white and its rather large collar is worn out over the collar of the jacket.

'Contracts?'

She is always dressed like this, in a dark suit, navy or black, chalk or pin-stripe, sometimes a skirt, sometimes trousers. She never wears a coloured blouse, always white or cream.

'Contracts.'

'Oh yes,' he says, remembering. 'I haven't signed them yet, but I have them here in this folder,' and he goes over to his desk, where he notices a letter that had arrived in the morning's post. 'By the way, would you have a look at this?' He pushes the letter across to her and it buys him time. He could always ask Imelda, couldn't he? Imelda, who can fire people with the same insouciance with which an abattoir worker can kill a pig. Imelda, who doesn't like novels or films because they're made up. Imelda, who probably didn't believe in Santa even when she was a nipper. He could always ask her. *Imelda, have you ever looked at a female Garda and found yourself imagining her in her pyjamas? Have you ever heard the erotic memories of an elderly relative echo around the room? Do people on the DART ever appear to you to be dead?* Yes, he could always ask Imelda, but what would be the point?

She finishes reading the letter and pouts. 'It's what I expected. It'll be a challenge.'

'You mean it'll be difficult.'

Imelda frowns at him, not getting it.

'What about those contracts?' she says yet again. 'Jesus, Fintan, wake up! Wake up!' and she leans over the desk, snaps her fingers twice sharply, just under his nose.

'I am awake!' Fintan cries hotly. 'I am!' He takes out his fountain pen with its white star on the end of the cap, and he signs his name again and again, *Fintan Buckley, Fintan Buckley.* It soothes him. He feels the give in the nib of the pen. The black ink is wet as he loops the letters. *Fintan Buckley, Fintan*

Buckley. That is me. He lifts his head and gazes into Imelda's eyes, troubled by what has happened between them, and trying to connect. She stares back at him blankly.

'I don't know how you're bothered with a pen like that. The ink takes ages to dry.'

A	s Fintan is crossing the landing that evening Niall calls out from his room, 'Dad? Is that you?'
'It is,' he says, and he puts his head around the bedroom door.

'I've got something for you.'

Fintan, who has only just returned from work and is still carrying his briefcase, steps into his son's bedroom rather shyly. It is a place he rarely visits. This is partly out of respect for Niall's privacy: he is acutely aware that both his sons are grown men. Unlike Colette, he feels that the sooner they are out of the house and gone, the better for everyone. It is also for the more practical reason that Niall's room is so small, and so packed with things, that there is barely room for two people to be in it at the same time.

Niall's is the smallest bedroom in the house, no more than a box-room really, into which, obliging as ever, he had mildly agreed to move when they found out that Lucy was on the way, his old room becoming the nursery and then her bedroom. Niall's only request had been for built-in bookshelves, floor to ceiling, which his parents had provided with alacrity. These bookcases are another thing that Fintan dislikes about the room, for they make it tremendously claustrophobic: it is like being trapped in library stacks. He does not know how Niall sleeps in such a place. Fintan himself feels sure that he would have nightmares about the laden bookcases moving inexorably together, crushing him where he slept in the little narrow bed; it gives him the creeps even to think about it. Although it is stuffed with things it is the room of an ascetic, the room of a man for whom little matters more than the life of the mind. Books and music-related technology predominate. There is an open laptop on the desk, with a Renaissance painting as its desktop picture. The room is oddly lit. Apart from the glow of the computer screen, there is an angle-poise on the desk, and another small lamp clipped to one of the bookcases.

All at once, there is the confusion of feelings that the seeming poverty of his son's desires habitually triggers in Fintan. Impressed and humbled by Niall's frugality, there are also moments when he finds it irritating that he should be satisfied with so little, with his tatty paperbacks and shabby clothes. In fairness, it had been worse when Niall was in his early teens, when he had been a vocal and frequent critic of Fintan's own little pleasures, his Christmas cigars, his holiday lobsters. ('It's just a symbol, Dad, a symbol of luxury.' 'No, it's not, it's a glass of cognac. Now feck off and let me enjoy it in peace.')The only criticism these days was either implied or imagined.

'We should get you one of those fancy shed things,' Fintan says, as he sits down on the edge of the bed. 'Put it in the garden and give you a bit of space.'

'Oh, you don't have to go to that sort of trouble, this is fine,' Niall says vaguely, rummaging through a bag of books on the floor. 'Do you remember you asked me the other evening about early colour photography? I've been looking into it for you. There's a ton of stuff online, but I know you're kind of old-school, so I got some books out of the university library.' He hauls them out and clears a space on the desk, sets them down. 'You sort of did me a favour asking about it, because it's something I didn't know much about, and it's actually very interesting.'

'It was Lucy who made me think about it,' Fintan says, and

he recounts the anecdote of her asking about the change from black-and-white photography to colour, attributing it to a change in the world itself.

'She's a philosopher, that kid,' Niall says, and he laughs 'She's always saying things like: "Where does the past go?"'

For the next half-hour or so, until called to dinner, they leaf through the books and look at the photographs. Niall points out how photography started by trying to mimic paint-ing—there are portraits, landscapes, still-lifes and nudes—just as the movies started out by trying to ape drama. There are pictures of lemons and trout, pale eggs in a blue bowl, biscuits and studies of flowers. What strikes Fintan—and he hesitates to say this to Niall, for fear of sounding foolish—is how alarm-ingly familiar all these things look, exactly like eggs and bis-cuits, fish and flowers which he might come across on any day of his life.

Niall explains the technical side of it to Fintan as best he can: how there are several different types of colour processes, and both of them are particularly impressed with one of the earliest, Autochrome. Niall shows Fintan how it employed grains of potato starch to make blobs of colour, and how this then operated like pointillism, the tiny specks of colour inter-acting to give the illusion of reality.

'It's like pixels in a digital photo, you know?' he says. (Fintan doesn't know.) 'But what I can't figure out is that it's quite a crude system—look closely, for example, and you can see the individual specks of colour with the naked eye. You'd think then that the photos themselves would be poor quality, but they're not, they're amazingly sharp.'

Fintan doesn't agree. It is the strange combination of accu-racy and a kind of softness that he finds so appealing in the Autochromes. He finds himself imagining, until Niall inadver-tently pulls him up, that this is how life would have looked before the First World War. 'It washes everything in this kind of buttery light, doesn't it, and then we get all kind of nostalgic because we know what was ahead of these people. The whole illusion of reality is very attractive, isn't it?'

'Yes,' Fintan wants to cry, 'yes it is.' He wants to warn these people in the photographs, to save and defend them. the little boys for whom the trenches of northern France are waiting; the babies who will come of age in the first half of the twentieth century. There is an Edwardian girl with her parasol, her white muslin dress and coiled, elaborate red hair. Fintan finds he can believe in her, identify with her as he could not with the people in the black-and-white photos he had seen in the cafe some days earlier. The colour makes a difference that he could not have imagined; it is almost shocking to him.

'And isn't it interesting,' Niall remarks, 'just who gets photographed? A pity, too. The bourgeoisie, the aristocrats. You only get one side of society, in the main.'

'What I like,' Fintan says, 'is the way photographs like this stop time.' Niall, who had been slowly turning the pages, stops and looks sideways at him in surprise.

'But they don't,' he says. 'How could they? You'll be telling me in a minute that they look real.' Fintan says nothing, stumped as to how he might explain to his son the complex of ideas and emotions that the photographs open up for him. But Niall understands and he laughs. 'They're just a construct, Dad. A kind of, like, an idea of reality, not "reality" itself,' and he hooks invisible punctuation marks in the air with his fingers. 'How could they be?' he asks rhetorically, before starting to turn the pages of the book again.

There is a small calendar above the desk where he is sitting, and in the square for the date three days hence is written 'Catherine 4:00 P.M.' Fintan does not know who Catherine is. Colette had been annoyed with Fintan some time back when he remarked to her his surprise at how popular both their sons seemed to be with girls.

'Why wouldn't they be popular? Aren't they both great fellows?'

Fintan knows almost nothing about this side of Niall's life. At times he wonders how much even Niall himself knows about it. Ever since he was in his mid-teens girls had been drifting in and out of the house in his company. Niall had often appeared to be surprised by their presence, even as he made them pots of tea and put out biscuits, as if they were the human equivalents of stray cats who had followed him home, and kindness suggested that they be offered refreshment. Lovely young women they were too, confident and bright, always full of chat. It mystified Fintan as to what they saw in his younger son, so lacking in dynamism, so dreamy and vague.

He finds Rob's intimate life similarly baffling. His rather cynical personality, his rationality and ambition might have suggested a somewhat cold approach and a succession of trophy girlfriends, leading eventually to a trophy wife. But in Freshers' Week at UCD Rob met Mags, a garrulous girl with an infectious laugh, hair the colour of toffee and a gap between her front teeth: they have been together ever since. Although he is extremely fond of her, Fintan veers between wondering what Mags sees in Rob and what Rob sees in Mags. Colette, more shrewdly, understands perfectly the dynamic at work and knows that Mags will most likely be the mother of her grandchildren. She knows, too, not to speak to Fintan about this, that it would only bewilder him.

'What I find hard to believe,' Fintan says, struggling to articulate what it is about the photos that astonishes him, 'is that if someone from a hundred years ago were to walk into this room now they would look exactly the same as we do. I think,' and it is suddenly revealed to him, 'I think that I was making exactly the same mistake as Lucy, without even realising it: I also thought that the world was black and white in the past. Of course I knew it wasn't, but I couldn't get past what the photographs seemed to present.'

'Black and white,' Niall says, laughing, 'and slightly out of focus and fuzzy at times.'

Now Fintan has it exactly.

'I was confusing the technology with what it was recording.'

'As if you thought people in the past had crackling, scratched voices when they sang, like the recordings on that old horn gramophone Auntie Beth has in her house. But look at it this way, Dad,' Niall continues. 'You're old enough to remember the past—not the First World War, obviously. No, but seriously, think about your childhood. You must be able to remember things from, say, the sixties, in a way that's different to how they look in photographs from that time and that are unlike anything you'd see nowadays.'

In a most uncharacteristically obliging manner, Granny Buckley immediately presents herself to Fintan in his mind's eye, dressed for Sunday Mass, in a black wool coat that comes almost to her ankles. The coat has a collar of curious ridged black fur to which is pinned a brooch in the shape of a wish-bone, embellished with a pearl and a small garnet. Her shoes are black leather, laced up and close-fitting, with blocky con-cave heels; and her hat is a dome of black felt, adorned with a bunch of hard fake cherries which are absurdly shiny and bright. From beneath this hat Granny Buckley's little face, all parchment skin and age spots, peers out, unsentimental and hard. This is exactly how she looked and dressed when Fintan was about six—younger even than Lucy is now; and yet she seems to exist in the same time continuum as his colleague Imelda earlier in the day, with her business suit and her pale blouse—that is, the reality of both women is convincing to Fintan.

'Yes,' he says to Niall, 'I take your point. I see what you mean.' From his briefcase he takes the two photographs that

Martina had loaned him, and sets them on the desk. Niall laughs when he sees the young woman with the straw hat, lounging in her chair.

'She looks really hot!' This is a thought that Fintan himself has not wished to acknowledge until now, given that the woman is a long-dead relative and looks very like his own sister. 'Has Rob seen this?'

'He hasn't, no.'

'Has Martina?'

'It was Martina who gave it to me, and she also gave me this. It was taken up north with my father's family.'

'Oh this is so cute,' Niall says, 'with the horse and everything. You must show this to Lucy, she'll love it.' He moves the photo under the light of the lamp, the better to see it. 'Tell me who the other people are. I recognise you and Martina, but who's the other boy?'

'That's my cousin Edward.'

'And that's your dad's mum?'

'That's Granny Buckley, yes. Don't be taken in by the fact that she's laughing and looks quite jolly: she was as tough as an old boot. I liked her, though,' he adds, surprising himself. 'She was kind-hearted underneath it all. I think women's lives were very hard in those days, especially in the country, and they had to be tough to endure it.'

'How did she get on with Joan?' Niall asks.

'She didn't.'

'Why does this not surprise me? It's a pity your dad isn't in the picture. You hardly ever mention him; what was he like?'

'He was wonderful,' Fintan says with feeling. 'I might not talk much about him, but there's not a day goes by that I don't think about him. He was actually quite like you, Niall, very gentle and sweet-natured.'

'Was he away to be a priest at one stage, or did I imagine that?'

'No, no, you're quite right. He went to the seminary in

Maynooth, and I don't think Granny Buckley ever forgave him for leaving it two years later. It was the old story, he always used to say: she was the one who had the vocation, not him. He couldn't go back to live at home again, so he stayed in the Republic and trained to be a teacher. It was seen as a bit of a disgrace in those days, to go off to be a priest and not to stay the course. Whatever about his mother, I don't think he ever quite forgave himself for dropping out. Martina always says'— he hesitates and then decides to press on—'Martina always says that he married Joan to sort of punish himself for the priesthood not working out.' He regrets this rather mean-spirited remark as soon as it is out of his mouth, most particularly as he has given Martina full ownership of it, instead of honestly claiming the sentiment for himself.

'Poor old Granny!' Niall protests. 'She isn't as bad as all that!'

'I didn't say she was,' Fintan replies, trying to backtrack. 'Herself and my father weren't a good match, that's all I'm saying.'

'Were you there in the seventies?' Niall asks, looking at the photograph again. 'When the Troubles were on?' Fintan explains what the situation had been and tells him about the subsequent falling-out. 'You can't blame Granny,' Niall says. 'I mean my granny, that is: Joan.'

'It wasn't really dangerous where we were, out in the country.'

'So there was nothing at all? Absolutely nothing?'

Fintan thinks for a moment.

'There were soldiers around,' he says. 'Quite a lot of them at times; we used to get stopped at checkpoints when we were out in the car with my uncle. Once we were caught up in a bomb-scare.'

'And you're telling me,' Niall says, 'that you would let Lucy go to a place like that?'

Fintan stares at his son.

'Don't be ridiculous,' he says. 'Of course I wouldn't. Not in a million years.'

'Poor old Granny,' Niall says again. 'Everyone's always so unfair to her.'

Now they can hear Colette downstairs, calling them to dinner. As Fintan stands up, Niall hands him the two photographs, with a last lingering glance at the sepia portrait and a somewhat wistful laugh.

'*Où sont les neiges d'antan*, eh Dad?'

But Fintan has no idea what he is talking about.

EIGHT

As she drives across town, Colette remembers walking down Grafton Street with Fintan all those years ago, and him suddenly saying, 'Let's go in here a minute,' and dragging her into Switzers. She didn't know why—generally he hated shopping, and she was more baffled still when he walked purposely through to the cosmetics department, heading for the counter of one particular concession. Colette had felt ill at ease then, had wanted to leave, because she found such places intimidating, with their perfectly groomed and condescending staff; was always afraid of being bullied into buying an expensive pot of face cream that might help her complexion but would ruin her modest budget.

Fintan walked fearlessly up to a sales assistant of exceptional beauty. She was wearing a white coat, with the name of the brand she was selling embroidered on it in red. Before Colette had a chance to read the name on the small gilt name badge, pinned above the embroidery, the woman spoke, and she recognised the inflection of her voice, the familiar tones, and was astonished to realise who this must be. Fintan confirmed it immediately.

'Colette, this is my sister Martina; Martina, Colette.'

What did Colette expect? Amused pity. But it wasn't what she got, although Fintan told her later, years later, that he too had feared that that might be the response. When they were teenagers, sabotaging his chances with girls had been a favourite pastime of Martina's: sniggering when he brought home his latest crush, pulling faces and crossing her eyes when the object of his affection had her back turned, and generally undermining his virtually non-existent love life in the way only a younger sister can.

'I like your scarf,' Martina said to her, surprising Colette that she might admire anything about her attire. 'It's real silk, isn't it?'

'I think so. I got it for Christmas.' As soon as she said this she thought herself foolish; it was like something a child might say, but again Martina didn't choose to be condescending.

'It's a great colour, very unusual. Anything here I can interest you in?' and she gestured to the display of creams and cosmetics before her. 'Anything you'd like?'

'Oh no, I never wear makeup,' Colette replied and at this Martina did give a sly smile.

'I suppose Fintan told you he doesn't like women wearing makeup, eh? All men say that and it's guff. They don't realise that you are wearing makeup, if you put it on properly. This stuff really is good, and you have to have a few little treats, I insist.' She took a small carrier bag and pulled out a drawer below the counter, started to select what seemed to Colette like a great many samples and sachets, which she dropped into the bag.

'How are things with you anyway, Fintan?' she asked as she worked at this task. 'How's college? Have you taken Colette over to meet our lovely mother yet?' Even Colette, whose purity of heart had inured her against most irony, even she could sense the subtext here, and she saw for the first time on Fintan's face a look with which she is familiar to this day: the narrowed eyes and the wry set to the mouth, the look he uses to silence and to warn, most usually when Niall or Rob say something in front of Lucy which he would rather that she did not hear.

'Not yet,' he said evenly, 'but we did call to see Christy and Beth a couple of Sundays ago.'

And with that it was Martina who suddenly appeared child-like, looking up from the drawer, all irony gone. 'I love Christy and Beth!' she cried wholeheartedly. 'And isn't their house just the nicest place ever? All those funny woolly pictures, and the cat, and that thing for the music with the big golden horn? And they always make you tea, and even if you're fed up when you go there, you're always happy by the time you leave. Oh they're just the best! I'm glad you met Christy and Beth.' She pushed the drawer in with her hip and handed the carrier bag to Colette. 'I have stuff here for men too,' she said to Fintan, 'but you're a lost cause, you fat old badger.'

Oddly enough, Martina was mistaken in this; or at least, Colette thinks, Fintan has changed a lot in the years since then. He has become very particular about grooming, with a taste for expensive aftershave, and an impressive collection of cufflinks about which his sons rib him all year, but to which they add at Christmas and on his birthday.

When she arrives at the shop today Martina is serving someone. Another customer is browsing through the racks, and there is someone behind a curtain in one of the changing rooms. Sitting on the counter is a turquoise carrier bag, tied shut with a dark-brown grosgrain ribbon, and with the name of the boutique, Chocolat, written in the same colour on the side of the bag. The customer is tapping the number of her credit card into a machine, and Martina takes advantage of this to smile over in greeting at Colette, who smiles back and turns away to look at a rack of dresses, to indicate to her sister-in-law that there is no rush.

Colette has no great confidence that she will find something that suits her, as least not without help. She knows that Fintan thinks she always puts comfort above looks, but that isn't strictly accurate. She has never felt at ease in her own body, has never seen it as something to adorn and enjoy, as Martina clearly does. Colette may see clothes and accessories that she likes, scarves and pieces of costume jewelry, but she does not know how to put them together as a 'look.' This is strange, given how good she is with her domestic space, for in another life she might have been an interior designer or a stylist. She has an unerring instinct for what might look right in a room, for choosing furniture, lamps, rugs and pictures which all enhance each other, to create something elegant and harmonious. But when it comes to dressing herself, all that skill and taste mysteriously vanishes, and she succumbs to clashing colours, to garments that are in themselves perfectly fine, but the cut or fabric of which is unsuitable for her build or complexion.

The only time Colette has been fully at ease in her own body was when her sons were born. She had felt like an animal then, but in a good way. Even when Lucy came along it hadn't been the same, because she hadn't wanted a third child. This is something she doesn't like to admit to herself, even now. But with Rob, and then Niall, she had felt like a thing in a lair, in a nest; instinctive, elemental; and she thinks that it would hardly have surprised her then had she found her whole body covered in thick fur—certainly it wouldn't have bothered her. Sometimes, even now, she looks at Beth and Martina's tabby cat, poised and sculptural, and she envies it its neat coat, the fan of fine black lines in the fur on the top of its head, the elaborate tortoiseshell markings on its curled and sleeping back. What need of clothes when one looks so fine in one's pelt?

The first customer has left, and the browsing woman approaches the counter with several garments over her arm: a skirt and two blouses. As Martina wraps them in tissue paper for her the woman praises the shop. She says it is the first time she has been there and asks if it has been open for long.

'A good few years now,' Martina says. 'I lived in London for a long time. I was a buyer there, in one of the big stores, and then when I moved back to Ireland I started this place.'

When the customer has left the shop, Martina is at last free to come out from behind the counter and greet Colette properly. She is wearing a grey linen dress over a white blouse. The dress is a rather complicated garment, with many layers, tapes, and fastenings, and a ruched hem; the sort of thing which requires a certain style and confidence to carry it off properly. It looks casual but also elegant and sophisticated. She also has a grey-and-white scarf tied around her head, and her long hair is piled up within it, with a few loose strands escaping. She habitually wears her hair like this at work, and it reminds Colette, bizarrely, of small cakes she remembers from her childhood, that were baked within a straight-sided paper wrapper, with the cake piled up deliciously within. For all that, Martina's hair looks great, Colette thinks. It is a style she admires so much that she had tried once to emulate it at home, with a hilarious lack of success, her curls standing straight up above the scarf so that it looked as if she had her finger in the light socket; so that Lucy banged on the door of the bathroom where Colette had closed herself away for the experiment: 'Mummy, why are you laughing so much?'

'How are you?' She kisses Colette. 'And the kids? And that brother of mine?' Colette asks after Beth and they chat for a moment. Martina produces the two linen jackets about which she had spoken to Fintan, and the existence of which he had dutifully relayed back to Colette. One is blue and one is pink: 'A nice shade of pink,' Martina remarks, 'kind of raspberry,' and then she laughs. 'It's a good thing Fintan isn't here,' and then they both laugh, for they know that the way they talk about colours bewilders and annoys him, Colette proposing paint that isn't quite stone-coloured, more of a mink; and Martina describing garments with a terminology that is to him obscure and weird: magenta, teal, and tobacco.

Colette tries on the pink jacket. It feels a bit stiff to her in its newness, but she does like it. The colour has strength without being too bright, and she knows that the linen will soften up with wear.

The curtain of the occupied cubicle is suddenly drawn back and a woman emerges. She is exceptionally pale, and the beige slip dress she is wearing drains from her complexion what little colour there is. The low cut does her no favours either, making her breasts look like two unappetising blancmanges. The silk clings to her body; the outline of her big knickers is clearly visible. Colette stares at her. Even she can see that this is all wrong. This is car-crash fashion; this is a masterclass in how not to dress.

'What do you think?' the woman asks Martina. Martina stares at her for a moment with narrowed eyes and then she says, 'The first one was better. The purple one.'

'Are you sure?'

'Definitely. You looked marvellous in it.'

'I liked this one on the hanger,' the woman says, looking at herself sideways in a long mirror, 'but now that it's on, I'm not so sure. Maybe you're right. The other one sat better, didn't it?'

'It did, and the colour was perfect on you.'

'Very well then,' the woman says, 'I'll take the purple one.'

She retreats to the cubicle and pulls the curtain closed again. Martina mouths silently to Colette: *I told her! I told her!* Colette fights the start of a fit of the giggles, and Martina puts her finger to her lips, winks at her and then talks aloud about the possibilities of the raspberry jacket, of which clothes already in Colette's wardrobe might go with it, of pieces she might like to consider for the future. Martina is leading her across the shop to look at some dresses when the door opens.

A woman with a baby in a buggy attempts to come in, but no sooner are the front wheels over the threshold than Martina is there, friendly but firm: 'I'm so sorry, we don't allow buggies in the shop.' The woman is slightly disgruntled, but says she will park it outside, and just bring in the baby. 'I'm sorry, that won't be possible either,' Martina says, still firm but no longer friendly. 'It can't be allowed; I've had too much merchandise damaged in the past.' Colette is afraid the woman with the baby is about to start a fight, but although she is clearly annoyed now she is timid too, and yields to Martina, who holds the door open so that she can extricate the buggy. She thanks the woman formally, wishes her good day.

'Sticky little hands grabbing at my best stock. I don't think so,' she mutters to Colette as she resumes her fashion counsel. The woman emerges from the cubicle with the beige and purple dresses over her arm. Martina goes to the till and serves her, then Colette pays for the pink jacket and for a grey linen skirt she has also chosen on Martina's advice, and by that stage there are more customers in the shop. They promise each other that they will meet again soon for coffee, for a proper chat; and the bell on the door of the shop clangs as Colette leaves with her turquoise carrier bag.

* * *

Martina's boutique stands in a little parade of shops, all of them rather chic. There is an independent wine merchant's, a fishmonger's, an interior design shop which Colette forces herself not to enter, and a cafe, to which she does yield. The barista is banging coffee grounds out of the machine; there is a strong smell of vanilla. Colette orders a cappuccino, and from a series of thick glass jars on the counter she chooses a cookie, a thick, pale cookie with Smarties embedded in the top of it. The barista puts it on a plate for her, and says that a waitress will bring the coffee to her table.

Colette installs herself next to two women, similar in age to herself but more *soignée*. Who isn't? she thinks. As is so often the case in this circumstance, one woman is dominating the conversation while her companion listens and nods. On the rare occasion when she does speak, the second woman's voice is softer and lower than that of her friend. There is music on in the background, and the barista is still banging away.

Colette's cappuccino arrives. She cannot yet bring herself to eat the cookie. With its brightly coloured sweets it reminds her of the kind of thing she sometimes bakes with Lucy on rainy Sunday afternoons: cakes made of broken biscuits and melted chocolate; iced buns sprinkled with edible stars. Colette particularly enjoys these moments with her daughter, because they balance out somewhat the quotidian chores of child-rearing, the homework and the parent–teacher meetings, and the thought of which had made her resentful when she found out that another baby was on the way. Then when it turned out to be Lucy, everyone said how nice it would be for her to dress a baby girl, after two little boys, and that was a laugh, wasn't it, when she could hardly dress herself?

Just before Lucy started national school, Colette had presented her to Fintan and the boys one night after dinner, the little girl shy but pleased in her new grey gymslip, white blouse, and navy tie. Colette had seen Fintan's eyes fill up with tears, the big softie, and Rob cried, 'Who's this big girl? Where's Lucy gone? Who's this?' which made Lucy blush, and pleased her immensely. Niall said nothing.

But he said plenty ten minutes later, when he cornered Colette in the kitchen. 'A tie, Mum? A fucking tie? She's five, for Christ's sake. She shouldn't be wearing shit like this. She should be wearing crazy stuff at her age. That pinafore thing is gross.' And then Fintan had got stuck in, 'Don't you speak to your mother like that,' and suddenly they were in the middle of a full-blown family row, a rare thing for the Buckleys, particularly so when Niall was at the centre of it, Niall who, as Rob puts it, 'would make the Dalai Lama look aggressive.'

But allowing for moments like that, things have worked out well with Lucy, Colette thinks, picking a first Smartie off the cookie, a red one, and eating it. Two children would have been enough for her but three is good, and the older Lucy grows, the more Colette appreciates having a daughter. As for Fintan, she realises now that his life wouldn't have been complete without Lucy, whom he adores.

Sometimes Colette thinks he is overprotective of her. He is still bothered about arrangements for the sleepover with Emma, which is beginning to irritate Colette a bit. It's not the child's fault that her parents split up. Colette hasn't met Emma's father; and would admit that she finds Emma's mother a flighty woman, overly concerned with material things, but she has always been responsible in any dealings Lucy and Colette have had with her. Fintan is trying to come up with something other than a sleepover that will keep everyone happy. *Good luck to him*, Colette says to herself.

She had been a bit taken aback by the way Martina had dealt with the woman and the baby just now. It had struck Colette as a slightly chilling illustration of how her sister-in-law had changed over the years, something Martina herself had alluded to in a recent conversation, with more than a touch of bitterness, although Colette can no longer remember the context. 'You start out here in life,' Martina had said, holding her hand out to the right, as though giving directions, 'and you end up here,' indicating then in exactly the opposite direction. 'And this is how you get from here to here.' She moved her hand back to its original position, and then swept it slowly through a complete arc of one hundred and eighty degrees, all the time making infinitesimal chopping gestures to indicate the many compromises, accommodations and changes of opinion that led one eventually to a complete volte-face.

Oh maybe this was unfair. In many ways she was still the same old Martina, funny and generous and beautiful. She was still the same person who had been a bewitching presence at Colette's own wedding, when everyone had asked, 'Who is that girl? Who's the looker in the hat?' For she'd worn with aplomb a huge tilted disc which she'd defined politely when asked as being made of polished straw. She'd gone off to live in London not long after that, and got out of the cosmetics business; started working in the fashion trade, something which she'd often said she'd like to do. Joan had been impressed with neither the career move nor the change of location, but then, little that Martina did seemed to please Joan. Colette herself is something of a favourite with her mother-in-law, which embarrasses her, given how hard Joan is on her own daughter, and for no reason that Colette can see.

Things had worked out well in London, at least to begin with. Martina clearly loved her new life, and on her trips home, which developed into a regular twice-a-year pattern over the ten years or so that she was there, she always came across as happy and relaxed. When the boys came along she was a better aunt at a distance than most would be as a constant presence. She sent home baby clothes that even Colette could see were of exceptional quality and charm, and as Rob and Niall grew she showered them with gifts: stuffed animals, bears and rabbits and cats; a wooden Noah's Ark; a perfect little toy farm. Martina spoke to the boys on the phone every week so that when she came home she didn't seem a stranger to them; and at Christmas they looked forward to her arrival as much as Santa's.

Colette indicates with a raised finger that she would like another coffee. The woman at the next table is still talking, her companion still listening and nodding, throwing in the occasional quiet comment; and Colette wonders, Do I do that? Do I dominate conversations in this way? Do I talk over Martina or Beth when I'm in their company? Most everyone who knows Colette would find this an absurd worry, but she resolves to be alert to it in the future. The waitress brings a fresh cappuccino to her table.

But by the time Lucy arrived, something had changed. Martina had been living back in Ireland about three years by then. She had come home unexpectedly, for a holiday, she said, in what turned out to be that fateful summer; and so it happened that she was there for Beth when Beth needed her. And then, almost immediately, Martina decided to stay. She insisted that she had already been thinking about it, that it had never been her plan to remain in London for the rest of her life. It was a lonely old city when it came down to it, she said; exhausting and expensive. It was all very well when you were really young, but she was in her mid-thirties now and she'd had enough. She wanted to be nearer her family.

All of this had sounded plausible to Colette at the time. She can remember noticing that Martina was unhappy; that her face in repose had a look of sadness that hadn't been there before, but she put that down to what had happened to Christy. Why, they'd all been sad about that; they'd all been vexed on Beth's account. But Martina had looked after her, and moved in with Beth at Beth's invitation. She started to look for work, and then she had a great stroke of luck: she found a backer in Dublin to help her open her own boutique. She sold the apartment she had in London and put the money into her new business. Within a year or two she was well established in a life which was, in its own way, stable and contented, but which was also, when you thought about it, far removed from the life Colette would have predicted all those years ago for the beautiful young woman in the polished-straw hat as she entered middle age: unattached, childless, living with her elderly aunt in her aunt's house.

When Lucy was born, Colette had been surprised, and rather hurt, at how little interest Martina showed. Certainly there were gifts, and occasionally visits to the house rather than phone calls; but it all felt perfunctory, had an air of duty always, rather than of love. She tolerated having Lucy on her knee if Colette or Fintan placed her there, but it was not an experience she sought out, and she would hand the baby back as soon as it was feasible to do so. Something had clearly changed since Rob and Niall had been small, and for a long time Colette was puzzled as to what it might be.

But when she did finally think of a reason she backed off immediately. She did not want to believe that she might be correct. For all that, it is highly plausible, given Martina's unease around Lucy, and her sudden flight from her life in England. Sitting now in the cafe, Colette cautiously revisits this idea in her mind.

Why should it not be true? It was reality for thousands of women every year but it was almost never spoken about, as least not to Colette. Pretty well every other trauma or misfortune she can name she can link to a personal circumstance: the woman who lived three doors up who had killed herself; the hairdresser's brother who had been murdered; the father of Rob's best friend in primary school who had been jailed for embezzlement. She cannot bear to think of Martina in those circumstances, feeling checkmated by life and having no-one to turn to—if what she imagines is indeed the case. The loneliness of it appals her. Time and again Colette has asked herself why she feels so strongly that what she believes about Martina must be true. She has no proof. If asked to justify her thoughts she could claim only an intuitive sense of Martina having been profoundly wounded as a woman. She sees this manifested in flashes of bitterness; in sudden cold or sharp remarks. Sometimes Colette even thinks that the way Martina dresses has something to do with it. Certainly she had always been interested in style, and had chosen her clothes with attention and flair. But Colette has on occasion a sense now of Martina armouring herself against the world; of constructing a carapace to protect herself, to console her body for whatever affront it has suffered, to negate it, and perhaps even to deny that such an affront has taken place. There is something about the way she presents herself that amounts almost to a scrupulosity.

Two years ago, Fintan and Colette had hosted a barbecue

for Joan's birthday, and invited the whole family. Early on, Colette and Martina had withdrawn from proceedings, taking with them glasses of wine and a bowl of olives, to a bench halfway down the garden, from where they watched as the meal was prepared: Niall on salad duty with Lucy; Fintan lost in a haze of scented blue smoke, grilling sausages and steaks; Rob busy with crockery and drinks. Joan and Beth sat together under a dark-green parasol. As Colette and Martina chatted, Colette could see her sister-in-law studying everyone in turn with almost forensic attention. At last she took a sip from her glass, and said to Colette, 'A family is quite something when you think about it, isn't it?'

'I suppose so,' Colette had replied. 'It all depends on the family.' Colette had always found extraordinary in the Buckleys the remarkable intensity of their feelings, and the strength of their attachment to one another: Fintan and Lucy, Niall and Rob, Martina and Beth. Colette likes this slightly overheated quality, having herself grown up in a cool and detached household, with two brothers whom she now almost never sees and with whom she struggles to find common ground when they do chance to meet. When she married Fintan she was at first astonished by the degree to which the Buckleys were all constantly on each other's case, meeting, ringing each other up, circulating family news; but she has grown to like it and she now shares this trait.

'Sometimes I find it strange,' she said to Martina, 'when I look at the family—I mean the five of us—sometimes I can hardly believe that we've made this little team between us, Fintan and me. And the kids are great but each in their own way; they're all very different, and yet it all holds together as a unit. The boys are pretty well adults now. I don't always agree with things they say or do, but I trust them. They'll move away into their own lives before long. Empty nest, and all that, though of course we'll still have Lucy with us for ages.'

'This will sound selfish,' Martina said, 'but I dread losing Beth. I know I lived on my own for years in England, but now I hate the prospect of it.'

Colette had tried to console her then with the example of Beth herself, and her late happy marriage to Christy, but Martina would have none of it.

'Never,' she said, and repeated it for emphasis, 'never. That side of my life is over. I want nothing more to do with men. I want to be left in peace.'

Colette had been taken aback by the vehemence with which she spoke, but it gave her an opening and she took it.

'Martina,' she said very softly, 'what happened to you in England? That time just before you came home? Do you want to talk about it?'

And Martina had turned to her, shocked, with a look in her eyes such as Colette thought she had never seen in anyone before. Martina hadn't answered Colette, but had put her wine glass down and stood up. She walked across the garden to where Rob was and started to talk to him, took a corkscrew from his hands and opened another bottle of wine.

Colette had been miserable for the rest of that day, thinking that she had annoyed and upset Martina, but when everyone was leaving Martina had whispered in her ear, 'It's very kind that you noticed, but I really don't want to talk about it.' She had then embraced Colette, who had hugged her back.

But it had troubled Colette ever since then to think of Martina going about with this great knot of unhappiness in her life, and there being seemingly nothing to be done about it. It troubles her yet, sitting here in the cafe, with the remains of her cappuccino cold in the cup before her. She looks at her watch. Time is moving on.

Before leaving, she buys another cookie studded with Smarties to take home for Lucy.

NINE

To a casual observer, Fintan's life throughout that spring would appear to be progressing in its habitual, unremarkable fashion. He takes the train into the city every day, and goes to the office, where he spars with Imelda and does his job with his usual indolent brilliance. He eats bigger lunches than he will willingly admit to when quizzed about it, by his concerned wife and teasing sons, over his substantial dinners at home in the evening. He ponders a suitable treat for Lucy and her little friend Emma, to compensate for the sleepover which he is still reluctant to sanction, and finally decides that the zoo might be a possibility; an outing so *déclassé* in these affluent and sophisticated times that it would have the added value of irony, were seven-year-olds able to appreciate such a quality. From time to time Colette nags him gently about paying a visit to his mother, something he knows is long overdue but which he can never quite bring himself to do.

And yet while all of this is happening, another reality has overtaken his life. Fintan has become obsessed with early colour photographs. Niall is complicit in this and feeds his habit, with books from the library, and links to websites which Fintan consults compulsively when he should be busy with his job, furtively minimising the screen should Imelda happen to put her head around the door for any reason.

He quickly grows technically proficient, and can easily distinguish the different processes; can distinguish an Autochrome from a Colourchrome with a casual glance. He is familiar with the names and works of pioneers in the field: the Lumière brothers, with their photographs of subjects more usually found in Impressionist paintings, such as bourgeois Belle Époque lunches in the open air; Lionel de Rothschild, with his family portraits and flowerbeds; and Albert Kahn, with his meticulous record of countries worldwide when their national stereotypes, long since homogenised and deconstructed by globalisation, had been the real thing. Perhaps most astonishing of all is the work of the Russian Gotkin, whose system of using three coloured filters gave results of almost alarming vividness and accuracy: it seems impossible that they can be so old.

Looking at the photographs makes Fintan feel vertiginous. They offer him a weird portal back into the past, into another world; as in the books he reads to Lucy at night, so that he feels as if he is tumbling slowly down a rabbit-hole lined with shelves, or that he has been shut into an open-ended wardrobe, pushing his way through furs and cool silks to a snowy landscape. On the day he first chanced to see the old photographs in the cafe, while eating his carrot cake, he had found it impossible to imagine himself back to that world. But now when he looks at the coloured photographs, which are sometimes barely a decade older than those black-and-white ones, he thinks—he, Fintan Buckley, hitherto a strong contender for the title of Most Unimaginative Man In Ireland—why, he feels that he might look up from his book and find himself back in the distant past.

'You wouldn't like it,' Niall says bluntly, when his father shyly confides this to him.

'Why not?'

'It wouldn't be the way you think.'

They're in the kitchen at home, on an overcast Sunday afternoon. Fintan is looking through one of his photography books while drinking tea and Niall has just wandered in, wearing jeans and a black T-shirt that says on it in tiny white letters, 'This is what I'm wearing today.'

'It would smell different, for a start,' Niall says, putting his hand to the flank of the teapot to gauge the heat of the tea, lifting the lid and peering in to judge the quantity. 'It would smell of horse piss and horse shit. I bet everything stank back then. Can I have some of this? Drains, people's teeth, you name it,' he continues, taking a mug from the cupboard and serving himself. 'But I'll tell you what I really can't stand,' he says, sitting down opposite Fintan. 'It's that sort of Heritage sense of the past. This girl I know in college, last summer she worked in one of those big houses that's open to the public. She had to dress up as a parlour maid and talk to all the visitors, tell them all this made-up crap. She said the room they liked best was always the laundry. But can you imagine what life really must have been like back then, doing the dirty work in a house like that? Can you imagine nursing someone with diarrhea in a house with no bathroom?' From the alarmed looked on his father's face, Niall knows that he's got the point he's making. 'They want people always to identify with the ruling classes,' he goes on. 'They want you to think as if it was always a summer afternoon back then, all croquet on the lawn and kids in white smocks and girls in big hats, all that kind of stuff.'

'There was such a reality,' Fintan says, gesturing to the open book on the table.

'Yeah, but come on, for how many people? It's not the whole story.' They sit in silence for a few moments, drinking their tea, and then Niall remarks, 'It's kind of interesting, though, to think about the past in this way, I mean the really distant past, 'cos photography is one of the things that makes the biggest difference.' He says to Fintan that the visual impact of visiting a new place must have been infinitely powerful if one had not seen in advance sharp colour photographs of it, 'and of course you couldn't see photographs like that at the time, 'cos there was no such thing.' He cites Goethe's nigh-on ecstatic account of visiting Rome at the start of the nineteenth century: the shock of the beauty of it; the strangeness.

Fintan doesn't agree. He says that no amount of documentary evidence had prepared him for the reality of seeing Venice for the first time. He says that Granny Buckley had described to him the arrival of the American soldiers in Northern Ireland during the Second World War, and how their second-hand familiarity—'They were like people in the films'—had only made them seem the more exotic.

'What I'm saying,' Niall argues, 'is that we tend to think that the past was more interesting than it really was, and my point is that it was more banal than we give it credit for, but also more complicated. And anyway, we're talking about "The Past" '—he makes quotation marks in the air around the words as he speaks them—'as if it was a discrete period of time, which is just stupid. I mean, if it comes to that, you can actually remember "The Past" '—he does the thing with his fingers again—'can't you, Dad?'

'Not a time before colour photography, no,' Fintan deadpans, and they both then laugh.

'But seriously, Dad, you must be able to remember things from ages ago, from when you were a kid?'

'It's very strange when I look at newsreels from the Troubles,' he says, 'because it does look familiar to me, and yet it also looks quaint: all the boxy little cars, the women in headscarves. But it wasn't quaint at all, it was bloody awful. I knew that, even when I was little. I remember being in Armagh with Granny Buckley one day, shopping, and we walked round a corner. There was a soldier coming the other way, holding a rifle, and he bumped into her. That is, the butt of his rifle hit her right in the solar plexus. The soldier swore—I think he said something like "Fucking hell!"—I don't exactly remember, but it was strong, whatever it was, because I was almost as shocked at someone swearing like that in front of Granny as I was at them nearly shooting her.'

'And how did she react?'

Fintan laughs. 'You have to hand it to Granny, she played a blinder. She said to him, "You mind your language, mister, and mind what you're doing with that thing." And then she swept on round the corner. But as soon as she was out of sight of the soldier she stopped and she leant against a wall and closed her eyes and she said over and over again, "Jesus, Mary and Joseph! Jesus, Mary and Joseph!" She was really shook, and it took a lot to rattle Granny. I mean when you think back on it, in one way it's kind of funny, and in another way it's horrific. And I'll tell you this,' he went on, 'I really do remember that as if it happened yesterday.'

'It's a strange thing, how memory works,' Niall remarks. 'I can remember you and Mum from the whole way through my childhood, from when I was small; and it seems to me in those memories that you don't look any different to how you do now. But if I look at photographs from that time, you look quite different. You both look much younger.'

Niall has finished his tea. He rinses his mug and leaves it on the drainer, then crosses to the window. 'Is it raining? I was thinking of going for a walk.' Fintan looks out into the garden, at Lucy's swing and the wooden bench.

'I don't think it's raining. It's hard to tell; it's a soft kind of day. I'd take a chance on it, if I were you.'

Niall drifts out of the room again, and Fintan continues to leaf through his book. He comes across a group of photographs from the First World War, of trenches and field hospitals, which are disconcerting because they look like stills from a film, even to him, who has always found historical movies unconvincing; the combination of period costume and the kind of teeth that only modern dentistry can provide striking him as particularly risible. He turns the page, and now he regrets that Niall has gone, because he has found a photograph which he would have liked to show him.

It is a picture of a red apple sitting on a mirror. There are other studies of fruit alongside, including a bowl of rather gnarled pears that look very much of their era, of a time before pesticides.

But the apple is perfect. It is one of those deep red, round apples, its skin so highly polished that the light reflects off it in a white spot. Apples have always been a potent fruit for Fintan, and not just because he loves eating them. They remind him of his childhood in the North, where his granny had a little orchard. The caption on the photograph states that it was taken in 1907, which Fintan can scarcely credit, so exactly does it look like something he might buy and eat with his lunch.

He glances up from his book and looks out of the window. It is definitely raining now, but it is a fine, soft misty rain, the sort you have to narrow your eyes and look closely at to be able to see it at all. The swing and the bench have disappeared, and the garden is full of apple trees. They are witchy and stiff; gnarled and sculptural; their branches ascending at first before inverting and pointing resolutely downwards. The colours are all drab, greys and shades of olive green. Fintan is aware now that he is actually sitting on the windowsill, which has become wider than it was before, as the window itself has become smaller and more deep-set; and Martina is sitting beside him, only she is a little girl. She is looking out into the orchard. 'Look,' she says. 'Look, Fintan. The trees are moving.'

She's right. Some of the trees at the back of the orchard have begun to move forward. Fintan and Martina watch without speaking. The moving trees continue to approach through the dankness of the day, and then Fintan says, 'They're not trees. They're soldiers.'

It's a foot patrol, in camouflage fatigues, and as soon as Fintan and Martina realise this, the illusion of trees vanishes.

As the soldiers draw nearer they can see them clearly: the metal helmets covered in net and all stuck with leaves; the blocky flak-jackets like perverse buoyancy aids, designed to make you sink; the long dark guns in their hands. They are moving closer, still somehow fitting in with the trees, in harmony with them, and yet also distinct now, as soldiers, as people. They are advancing inexorably towards the house. The sound of their voices is audible, the crackle of walkie-talkies. Fintan is afraid.

'Down! Down! Quick, before they see us,' Martina says, and she slides off the windowsill. As she goes, she grabs Fintan by the ankle and pulls him after her, so that he falls clumsily, and hits his head off the edge of the table with a tremendous bang, knocking himself out.

He opens his eyes. He is a middle-aged man, sitting at the kitchen table, not under it. There is a book, a mug and a teapot before him. In the wet garden there is a swing and a bench. Dizzy and unmanned, he is stunned, as if someone had closed the heavy book of photographs and brought it down hard on his skull.

TEN

S he looks in on Beth as she always does before leaving the house, quietly adding a jug of milk to the tray that had been set the night before: the bowl of cereal with a plate over it; the fruit; the cup inverted on its saucer; the tea-caddy; the little kettle. When she wakes, Beth will prepare her own breakfast and eat it in bed. Mid-morning, Martina will ring her from the shop to check that she's up and dressed, that everything's fine. But for now Beth is still fast asleep; and the cat too, curled in the crook of her knees. Martina withdraws and carefully closes the bedroom door.

She reaches the shop at eight-thirty. She raises the external electric shutter with a key; and as soon as she opens the door and goes in, the alarm starts to beep. She hurries through to the stock-room at the back to tap in the security code and immediately the beeping stops. Now she can relax. She walks back into the main body of the shop, and savours the silence.

Martina looks at herself in one of the many large mirrors provided for the customers. Today she's wearing an olive-green silk dress, simply cut, with an amber necklace. It looks perfect, she thinks, and the shop is perfect too. Recently refitted, it is all pale wood and chrome, with new racks designed to make it easy to put together an outfit: co-ordinating pieces are displayed beside one another, together with accessories, scarves and bags. It always astonishes her that many of her customers, including her own dear sister-in-law, fail to pick up on this rather obvious guidance.

No matter where she has worked, Martina has always loved this moment of being in a shop just before it opens, just before she moves fully into her professional persona. She is sensitive to the theatrical nature of what she does; is aware of it every night as she selects from her own wardrobe what she will wear the following day. She likes the slight distance there is in her dealings with the public, enjoys constructing a self for the customers to encounter.

By evening time, when the shop closes, it will be in disarray. There will be empty hangers, garments replaced in the wrong sections or displayed askew, the wooden floors will be grubby and scuffed; but this does not bother her. Before going home she will put everything to rights, and tomorrow morning it will all begin again.

The family doesn't appreciate what an accomplishment it has been for her, opening this shop and making such a success of it. She's always proud when it's mentioned in magazine features as being a special place: somewhere with exceptional stock; hard-to-find labels; things that you can't buy elsewhere in Ireland. It had always been her dream to have her own shop, but while she was living in London it had never been a possibility. Well, it had all worked out, in spite of the circumstances that had brought her home. She pulls her mind back from that line of thought, as she habitually does.

In the storeroom at the back of the shop she makes herself a cup of green tea, and as she drinks it she thinks about last night. She's sorry now that she loaned Fintan those photographs. She would have liked to have had them at hand yesterday evening, for she would have liked to look again at the picture of Edward, after having spoken to him.

She'd always liked him. Even as a child he'd been steady and sensible in a way she admired: he wasn't a cry-baby like Fintan, nor an imp like herself. She remembers playing cards with him on wet afternoons; remembers him giving her a robin's nest to take back to the city. There'd been something slightly courtly in his country manners, a formality that had appealed to her, and made him seem always older than he was.

He served at Mass. The first time she saw him up on the altar, walking out from the sacristy behind the priest in the company of two other little boys, she'd started to laugh, and Granny Buckley had had to smack her on the knee to make her stop. She hadn't laughed because she thought it was funny, but because it was strange, so incongruous; in the same way that she'd laughed when she saw Fintan on stage in the school nativity play, dressed as a shepherd. Edward's ecclesiastical duties had become more familiar to her, but they never lost their particular glamour, and she watched him closely as he snuffed out candles, as he generated clouds of incense from a smoking thurible and rattled the chain of it.

Last night when she'd gone to ring him, she'd misdialled at first and got a wrong number. An old man had answered the phone, and she'd quickly ascertained her mistake, but the old man had been uneasy. She'd understood his anxiety and guessed that he was living on his own, was fearful of burglars and confidence-tricksters. She told him she'd been trying to ring her cousin, she'd reassured him, and then he said in the soft accent she remembered from her childhood, 'That's grand, Daughter. Goodnight.'

She'd been strangely moved when she hung up. No-one had called her 'Daughter' in that way, as a term of endearment, for so many years now that she had even forgotten this partic- ular usage. It made her feel that the old man to whom she had spoken was close geographically to the old home-place but dis- tant in time; as if the phone had allowed her to communicate with someone who was still living in that world she had known as a child; as if he were one of the old farmers who had knelt beside her in the pew, as she watched Edward ringing a small golden bell.

The last time she saw Edward was at her own father's funeral, when they were both teenagers. Her own wild grief at that time she might have expected, given her attachment to her father; but there had been a surreal quality to those days that she could never have predicted. And one of the strangest moments had been at the graveside, for there was Edward walking towards her; but Edward as if he had been bewitched, as if the calm freckled child she had known years earlier had been conjured into this pale young man through whose kind but unfamiliar face she could see shimmer the look of her old companion.

There'd been a cautious mending of the relationship with her father's family over the years, but she and Fintan had never gone back after the end of their visits north in the early seventies, and their cousin had drifted out of their lives. Although they had all three been glad to meet again at the funeral, it hadn't marked a real resumption of their friendship. Too much time had passed. They were shy and strange with each other; awkward in the way of adolescence; and over the years it all dwindled into Christmas cards and stray bits of news—marriages, the births of children, Martina's move to England, the passing of Edward's parents. That was how things had stood for years now.

She rinses her cup and checks her watch, decides not to ring Fintan just yet, even though he, too, likes to arrive early, and will have been in his office for some time now. Martina doesn't know how her brother can stand his job, doesn't know how anyone can stand office life. Decades of looking at the same old colleagues, fiddling around with paperclips and photocopies: it seems even worse to her now than when she was eighteen. She might well have ended up in an office if Joan had got her way: she had wanted Martina to go to college when she left school. 'Selling lipsticks isn't much of a job, is it?'

Well it had been a very good job indeed, as far as Martina

was concerned, and right from the start she had loved working in a shop. She has never forgotten the words of her first supervisor: 'Remember, you're not selling cosmetics, girls, you're selling beauty.' Even today she considers that she is not selling dresses and jackets and skirts so much as she is selling confidence. She loves helping women to be all they can, coaxing them out of dowdy garments in drab colours and into more flattering attire. She loves dealing with customers who love clothes as much as she herself does, who have the knowledge to put together certain pieces to create a look which women with less style and audacity would never dare. They ask her advice. They confide in her. Women buy new clothes for all sorts of reasons. They're going to a party. To the races. To a wedding. They buy clothes because they feel good. They buy clothes because they feel miserable. They've fallen in love. They've been dumped. They've got a new job. They've been sacked. They've had a windfall. They're broke, but they still deserve a treat. Martina has seen women come out of the cubicle, look in the mirror and be shocked. She has seen them look in the mirror and be thrilled. She has seen wives step out of the changing room and husbands gasp. She has seen daughters step out of the changing room and mothers weep. Martina thinks that you have to have worked in a clothes shop to understand the depths of human emotion and pathos to be found there; to know the drama of it all.

She crosses to the window and looks out onto the street, sees the fishmonger from two doors up; and they smile and wave. All the traders in this little parade know each other. She's glad to be back in Ireland. It's not that she hadn't liked London, but she wouldn't have the energy for it now. The sheer volume of customers she'd had to deal with then in the big department stores where she'd worked had been of a different order; and then there was the city itself.

It had frightened her, to begin with, and she'd coped by

denying this, by not admitting, even to herself, how much the crowds appalled her. She knew why she was there: because she'd had more than enough of Dublin by the time she was in her early twenties. She'd been sick of her mother's criticisms; of going out with men only to discover that they had been at school with Fintan; of breaking up with boyfriends only to bump into them in town two days later. If the anonymity of London spooked her at times, it was also one of the things she had gone there to find.

'Do you miss London?' People were always asking her that, even now, when she'd been home again for so many years. 'Do you miss London?' She missed it today because it was a Thursday, and that had been her day off towards the end of her time there. She'd loved sleeping late, waking to the light in her own little apartment, taking her time to get washed and dressed instead of rushing for the Tube; and then going out for breakfast, drinking black coffee and reading the papers. She might go shopping herself later in the day, in the high-end stores in Bond Street or Knightsbridge; or meet friends for lunch. She has a great many happy memories from her time in London, from parts of the city she had grown to love: the lights of the Embankment at dusk, the green-and-white striped deck chairs in the parks in summer, the theatres as the lights went down and the curtain rose. Wine bars and restaurants. Memories that were like bright stones you could keep, that you could take out and inspect and admire; hold them to the light; see them glitter.

To begin with she had enjoyed her job almost as much as her days off. She didn't have a lot of experience in fashion retail when she went there, but she was fortunate in her new colleagues, who helped her. She'd quickly made friends with two other girls, Sally and Nell, who had already been there for a while; and although their supervisor Miss McKenzie had been a bit stern at times, she hadn't been the worst. Martina had shared a flat in Camden with Nell for a couple of years; they'd used to go drinking and dancing with Sally.

But of course nothing stays the same forever. Sally had changed her job and then Martina bought her own little apartment. Nell got married and had twins, moved out of London to somewhere in the distant suburbs; Martina can't now remember the name of the place. She'd lost touch with Nell over the years; and although she still occasionally hears from Sally, who also married and had children but has since divorced, they haven't met for ages. Martina doesn't want to meet either of them again, but there are no hard feelings. It's just that she would rather remember them all as they were, back in the day on the shop floor, impeccable with their gilt name tags and high heels; drinking tea and laughing beside the grey metal lockers in the staff room, or out together for cocktails in some fashionable bar.

It's getting on for nine o'clock now. She goes over to the phone beside the till and rings Fintan, who picks up immediately.

'I'm glad it's you,' he says. 'I thought it might be my colleague Imelda. I hope there's nothing wrong.' It's an odd hour, she knows, for her to be ringing him.

'Do you remember that photo I gave you, of us in the North when we were children, with Granny and the horse? It set me thinking about Edward again, and last night I just decided I would ring him to see how things are.'

'I wouldn't have thought you would even have a number for him.'

'I rang directory enquiries.'

'And you got him?'

'I did, yes. I was speaking to his wife, Veronica, first, and then he came on the line. Oh Fintan, it was great, but it was so strange. He's the loveliest man. I felt that he was a stranger but that I knew him, if that doesn't sound crazy. We didn't talk to each other like strangers.'

'It would be incredible to see him again, after all these years.'

'Well, that's what he suggested, and that's really why I'm calling. He wants us to go up for a visit. He said he'd speak to Veronica about a suitable date, and I said I'd speak to you.'

'It would be incredible,' Fintan says again.

They discuss when they might go north, and Martina remarks, 'I don't know why we lost touch in this way, why we let things drift. Maybe it was partly due to my being out of Ireland for so many years.'

And then Fintan surprises her by saying hesitantly, 'I don't think I ever told you this, but I'm so glad you came home again from London. To live, I mean.'

'No,' she says, 'you never told me that before.'

'Because of the way it happened—I mean it was a confused period, maybe you weren't even planning to come back, so by the time I realised you were home for good you'd been here a while. I suppose I sort of took it for granted then. But I was thinking about it the other day and I realised how much I'd miss you if you were still away.'

'Ah, go on out of that; you managed well enough without me for years,' she says, trying to lighten the mood, but Fintan will have none of it.

'That was then. Time changes things, and at this stage in the game I can't imagine only seeing you once or twice a year. It would be just awful. The kids are delighted you're here, and you're a true friend to Colette.'

'If I'd actually had a sister I couldn't have been any closer to her,' Martina says, capitulating to his sincerity, matching it. She's glad they're speaking on the phone and not face to face, glad too when Fintan begins to back off.

'It's just something that came to me. I thought I might mention it to you.'

She thanks him, promises again to keep him informed about Edward, and they say goodbye.

She's very touched by what Fintan has just blurted out, even though she's been back in Dublin for quite a few years now. The family hadn't ever consciously registered her return or commented much upon it. Certainly it hadn't been lost on her that the only people who were sensible to there having been something wrong—seriously wrong—with the circumstances of her coming home were her in-laws: Christy, and then, much later, Colette. And as for Joan, she thinks with some bitterness, why, she wouldn't care if Martina left Ireland again in the morning, never to return.

To attempt to distract herself from her thoughts she goes into the storeroom, and brings out a carton of cashmere cardigans she hadn't been planning to put out yet. She might as well: there's room on the shelves, and it comforts her to see and to touch the pink and cream softness of the wool, the small, neat buttons. Perhaps she might put a couple of them aside for Colette to look at. Colette had once told her that Fintan wasn't just her husband but the only man she'd ever been involved with in her entire life. It hadn't greatly surprised Martina, indeed merely confirmed what she had sometimes thought might be the case. It did, on the other hand, make her grateful for the variety of her own emotional life. While she does on occasion envy Fintan and Colette everything they have together—their strong marriage, their children, the home they all share—she also at times thinks how tremendously boring she herself would find it all.

She stands by the life she has led, and she honours it. There's her career for a start: everything she achieved in becoming a buyer in London, and then the shop here in Dublin. Apart from a bit of temping and translation back in her twenties, Colette has never worked outside the home. Martina doesn't believe there's anything—no husband, no children—that could have compensated for the satisfaction she has had from her working life. And as for her relationships—

well, there have probably been more of them than was ideal, and she still doesn't know why none of them had finally developed into something permanent, but there had been great times in many of them and even the bad ones had never been that bad.

And the thing that had ruined everything, that hadn't even been a relationship, it had just been a disaster. Martina doesn't want to think about it, but the touch of the wool in the cardigans is reminding her now of that time. She is thinking of Christy handing her the rug and her taking it. She doesn't want to think of that time. Think of something else. Think of something else. She looks again at her watch. Nine-twenty. She could open ten minutes early. With luck someone will walk in off the street and distract her; cancel the rising panic she feels. Looking at herself in the mirror, she takes comfort again in the green silk dress and the amber beads. She wipes her eyes. Don't cry. Don't cry. She looks the part. Everything will be fine. She's ready to perform.

Crossing to the door, Martina turns over the small white wooden board hanging there—OPEN—and begins her day.

ELEVEN

There's a little unpleasantness when Fintan and Lucy arrive at Emma's house to collect her, because Emma isn't there.

'Didn't that man ring you?'

'What man?'

Emma's mother rolls her eyes. 'Her father of course. She's with him this weekend. He knows that you're taking her to the zoo because I heard Emma telling him about it on the phone. She's really looking forward to it, so don't let him talk you out of it.'

'Where does he live?'

She scribbles an address on a scrap of paper, adds a phone number at Fintan's request, and gives it to him. He goes back to the car with Lucy and calls the number, but it goes to voice-mail, so he decides to head straight over.

The given address turns out to be a white apartment block with neatly landscaped gardens. They ring the bell for number eight, and Lucy shrieks into the intercom, 'It's me, Emma!' A man's voice replies, 'First floor,' and they are buzzed in, go up in the lift. Stepping into the carpeted hallway, Fintan has the impression of being in a slightly creepy hotel, where anything might be happening behind the rows of closed and numbered doors. There is the sense of the presence of others—muffled music in the distance, the sound of voices, but there is no-one to be seen.

The door of number eight opens. Light and noise escape in

a sudden burst, and Lucy darts in before Fintan can stop her, past the man who has opened the door.

Standing before Fintan is Fintan himself. That is, a younger Fintan, in his early thirties, dishevelled and unshaven, wearing a navy towelling bathrobe, but Fintan to the life: with his dark hair, blue eyes and slight paunch; his face displaying (although Fintan would not know to define it thus) the same combination of high intelligence and an innocence so incorrigible that it can sometimes look like stupidity. It is, to Fintan, a horrible sight. It is like being forced to sit opposite a large mirror in a restaurant and watch oneself eat.

'I'm Conor,' says this other Fintan.

'I'm Fintan,' says Fintan. The other man closes his eyes and pinches the bridge of his nose hard, then opens the door wide.

'Come in,' he says. 'I'm afraid we're running a bit late.'

Fintan follows him through the hall and into a spectacularly untidy kitchen, where the two little girls are already standing by a vast open fridge. There is the sound of a television coming from another room. The kitchen, which is flooded with light from big windows, has a central island topped in granite, and is furnished with tall silver stools. Emma pours orange juice from a carton for herself and Lucy, before they scamper off together to the room where the television is. Like a man in a dream, Fintan observes all of this in dismay, but is powerless to do anything. He had told Lucy on the way over that they wouldn't be going in; that they would collect Emma and go straight to the zoo.

Amongst many other things there are two pizza boxes on the central island, with 'Pepperoni' scrawled on them in black marker; and a bowl of sodden breakfast cereal, which has stained brown with chocolate the puddle of milk in which it is sitting: the kind of unwholesome fare that Colette refuses to have in the house.

'Coffee?' the other Fintan asks, wandering over to a fancy

chrome machine on the counter. Again, like a man enchanted, Fintan feels that he cannot refuse.

'Sorry about the mug,' Conor/Fintan says. 'It's the only one that's clean.'

'No problem,' Fintan says, adding milk to his coffee from the Avonmore carton sitting open on the counter. Pooh Bear looks out from the side of the mug: the Disney Pooh, yellow and dumb in his bum-freezer red jumper. There is a sudden surge in noise from the television as Emma comes back into the room.

'Daddy, can I give Lucy a yoghurt?'

'You can do anything you want, sweetheart.'

Fintan watches the other man watch the little girl as she opens the fridge and rummages inside. There is a look on Emma's father's face that Fintan can scarcely endure: a kind of love, shot through with pain and longing and desperate need.

'Raspberry. Yummy! Yummy!' She pulls out a drawer and takes a spoon, goes back to the other room, to the television, with her father's eyes still fixed on her.

'Do you mind if I smoke?'

'By all means. It's your house.' Fintan watches as Conor/Fintan lights up. Again, the resemblance is unnerving. They sit in silence for a moment, and Fintan looks again around the kitchen. This is domestic chaos on an industrial scale. He can just about find space on the island for his Pooh mug amidst the wreckage of a week's worth of rushed break-fasts and lousy dinners. The jacket of yesterday's suit hangs over the back of a chair; the silk snake of the tie lies coiled on the floor beneath it. The apartment is so coolly minimalist in its design, and yet so unrepentantly squalid, that Fintan cannot help but admire the other man for his sheer chutzpah in hav-ing comprehensively trashed the place, as a revolt against being forced to live there. Fintan salutes his refusal to be reasonable; his rejection of this chilly box as his home.

'What are the girls watching?' he asks then, primarily for the sake of saying something. The other man ferrets out a plastic DVD case from the mess on the island and passes it to him. '*Stuart Little.*'

The second most famous mouse in the history of cinema looks out from the lid, preppy in his chinos and sneakers, with his incongruous rodent's face. Fintan turns the box over and reads the parental warning on the back: 'Contains scenes of mild peril.'

'It's a good movie,' Conor/Fintan says unexpectedly; and before he can help himself Fintan has replied, 'Yes, but *Babe* is better.' He is grateful when Emma's father does not reply ironically to this, but says, 'The pig one? Yeah, that's good too.' He picks up the DVD box from where Fintan has set it down on the granite island again, and gazes at it through his cigarette smoke.

'How do they do that, anyway?'

'Do what?'

'The mouse,' Conor/Fintan replies. 'Get it to wear trousers and shoes and stuff. Get it to talk. I mean, I know it isn't a real mouse—well, maybe it *is* a real mouse, like, a film of a mouse, and then they do something with computers, you know? What is it they do?'

'I have no idea,' Fintan says. He doesn't like to admit that he has never thought about this before now; that when he had watched the film at home with Lucy he had, in a way, taken Stuart at face value. 'I don't know much about computers.'

'I could come with you,' the other man says suddenly. 'To the zoo. We could all go.' Fintan says nothing but stares back at him in silent dismay. To spend all day around this woeful, stricken man would be like a penance for some terrible sin that Fintan doesn't remember committing. 'It wouldn't take me long to get ready.' This is so clearly untrue of his rank, unshaven companion that there is no point in Fintan even commenting on it. Fintan/Conor knows it too; admits as much by stroking his stubbly jaw. 'I don't get to see her very often,' he says. 'The next weekend I'm due to have her I have to go to London for a conference. Her mother won't let me make it up—I mean, she won't give me extra days for the days I'll miss.' Fintan goes on staring at him, mute with pity, until the other man capitulates. 'Maybe it would take me too long to get ready.' His voice is hesitant. 'Maybe I should stay here and try to get, like, sorted out.' He looks uncertainly around the kitchen.

'That might be an idea,' Fintan says. 'Plan a nice meal with her this evening, something she really likes, and get in another DVD. You know, maybe it's better to have a shorter amount of time with her, but for that time to be really good and enjoyable for you both.'

The other man laughs sarcastically. 'Yeah, quality time,' he says. 'I'm sick of people talking to me about quality time. Fuck that for a game of conkers.' He grinds out his cigarette on a dirty plate, gets down from his stool and walks over to the door of the room where the television is. Fintan follows him sheepishly.

'How's the film going, girls?'

'It's almost over, Daddy.' As they watch, the credits begin to roll on the enormous television screen. The music is upbeat and loud. Stuart and a little boy are brushing their teeth. Stuart and the little boy are dancing. Fintan finds himself once again suspending his disbelief where Stuart is concerned. Emma's father takes her back into the kitchen to get her ready to go out; to comb her tousled hair and give her money. She goes to fetch her trainers from her bedroom, and through a series of open doors Fintan catches a glimpse of a room all pinkly girly, with a net canopy over the unmade bed and a white feathered dream-catcher on the wall. When Emma is finally ready to go, her father enfolds her in his arms, with the same hungry, needy love that Fintan had observed earlier.

'You have a lovely time, Princess, and come home safe to Daddy soon, won't you?'

'We won't be too long,' she says soothingly, as though he were the child and she the departing parent. 'I'll bring you back a nice present.'

In the car the girls settle into the back, clipping themselves in, chattering about the movie; about whether or not yoghurts are nicer than Petit Filous and why pots of Petit Filous are so much smaller than pots of yoghurt; while Fintan sits there wondering if he is going to be able to drive, so overcome is he by what he has just seen. That a life might be so purgatorial and yet still have in it such things as *Stuart Little* DVDs and granite kitchen islands stuns him. He imagines seeing Lucy for only a couple of days every week, and that with a bad grace on Colette's part. He thinks of what it would be to come home in his suit, with his briefcase and his BlackBerry, night after night, to that empty apartment, with its big telly and shiny appliances; with its deserted pink room. He fights the urge to go back to the apartment and give the other man a hug.

* * *

The first thing that happens after they have bought their tickets at the zoo is that someone takes their photograph. It's been years since Fintan was here, not since Niall and Rob were tiny. He even has faint memories of visiting the zoo himself as a traditional First Communion day treat. Most Dublin men of a certain age have, like Fintan, in their family archive, photos of themselves in a little suit with short trousers, a rosette of white ribbon pinned to their lapel; and the background taken up by the lower reaches of a giraffe, or the considerable expanse of an elephant's rear end.

He finds that he enjoys the zoo much more than he had expected; certainly more than the two girls, who are both very much of their time and are already sated with extraordinary experiences, particularly Emma: 'I saw lions last year. In Kenya, on safari with my mommy. Lions and zebras.' They are not greatly impressed by the animals here: they glance in the enclosures and pens and then hurry on, while Fintan stands transfixed by a snowy owl: an explosion of luxurious white feathers from which stares out an eerie, bad-tempered little face. So much for Stuart Little, he thinks. Who needs a mouse in sneakers and chinos when real animals look like this?

The bongos astound him. He had not known until today that such a creature existed, and now here are three of them. What must it be to be a bongo? A kind of antelope, its hide is a sensational golden toffee colour, like nothing he has seen on an animal before, offset by a tuft of coarse hair, like a short mohican, running the length of its spine, and cream stripes on its flanks. The bongos are ambling around on their neat hooves, seemingly indifferent to their own beauty.

The zoo has been redesigned over the years, and Fintan is surprised at how few traditional cages there are; makes a mental note to mention this to Niall, who had been predictably unenthusiastic about today's outing. There is an attempt to mimic as far as is possible the natural habitats of the animals. Some of the animals have taken sly advantage of this and are lying low, uncooperative. The snow leopard has been provided with a stony outcrop under which it has withdrawn, where it is curled up sleeping, so far back that it is barely visible. Fintan thinks that the animals should consider themselves lucky that it is not his colleague Imelda who is running the zoo. He imagines her calling the snow leopard in for a meeting. *I'm afraid this doesn't appear to be working for us. We're going to have to refresh your position.*

In contrast, the Sumatran tiger is scrupulously working out the full terms of its contract. Enclosed behind a sheet of plate glass, it is pure energy; it is sudden death wrapped in orange and black fur. Even Emma and Lucy shriek when it roars at them, inches from their faces, before it turns and slouches away again.

By the time they have seen monkeys and flamingos and penguins and otters, and a great many other animals, they are all three ready for lunch.

Fintan loves chips, and the ones they serve in the zoo are the business, shovelled out generously; not like those ridiculously thickly cut ones he is always irritated to find on his plate in fancy restaurants, arranged to form a little crate. The girls are having sausages too.

'Are they organic?' Emma asks, and Fintan fights the urge to reply, 'Was last night's pizza?'

'I really don't know.' This is a lie.

'Mommy only lets me eat organic meat.'

'I'm sure she won't mind, just this once.' This is also a lie. It is, moreover, an act of male solidarity. 'Do you want salt? Vinegar?'

As they eat, he watches the girls. It makes him feel guilty to remember how annoyed he had been when Colette told him another baby was on the way. Rob and Niall were half-reared by then, and while he got on well with them, he didn't feel he'd been such a roaring success as a father that he had any desire to repeat the experience. Night feeds, nappies: the very thought had made him want to howl, and that was before any consideration of the financial implications. By the time the baby was due Colette had been much happier about the situation, but Fintan had still been uneasy and apprehensive.

From the first moments of Lucy's life, it had been a love such as he had never imagined. So beautiful! So soft! So new! So tiny! And one day when he leant over her and smiled, she smiled back. At him! Fintan Buckley! Her daddy! That she was a girl rather than a boy meant that she wasn't a challenge to him; she wasn't a machine-gun hail of question marks in the way his sons had been to him, much as he loved them. If Lucy was in herself a question, it was one of those strange, mystical Zen questions that Niall had once told him about, impossible questions to which there was no logical answer; questions that were answers in themselves. Lucy was the sound of one hand clapping. All he has to do is love her.

As he thinks this, he is looking at the other little girl, at Emma, who is for her own father the locus not just of a love similar to Fintan's for Lucy, but of a suffering of concomitant intensity. She is frowning with concentration now as she squeezes ketchup out onto her chips, but she often frowns, Fintan has noticed. She does not have Lucy's levity of spirit. The fractured marriage of her parents has left its mark.

'I'll take you home to your daddy after this.'

But the girls are having none of it. They want to go to the little farm; they want to go to the shop.

They see the baby animals: the piglets, the chicks and the lambs. They go to the shop where they buy trinkets and toys. Lucy chooses two brightly coloured lollipops for her brothers. *Yes, Niall,* Fintan thinks, *there are additives in them, and who knows what else. If you ask me, they look as if they might be radioactive.* Emma buys her father a zoo mug with a picture of a gorilla on the side of it; and, for his office, some pens, a rubber and a pencil sharpener, which are, if anything, more colourful than Lucy's lollipops.

As they leave, they see that the photograph taken on their arrival has been printed up with a colourful frame, 'Dublin Zoo, 2006,' and is available to buy. The girls are unimpressed, but Fintan insists on having it as a souvenir.

And then they head for home.

* * *

The door of apartment eight is opened by someone Fintan

has never seen before in his life: a rangy man, skinny, even; with strawberry-blond hair and a pale complexion, with none of Fintan's ruddiness. This stranger greets Fintan as if they have met previously; and Emma addresses him as 'Daddy.' He insists that they go in for a moment, and when Fintan says hesitantly, 'Thanks, Conor,' the other man replies, 'No worries, Fintan.'

In their absence, Conor has clearly tried to put a shape on things. He's washed, shaved and dressed himself. The granite island has been cleared, and there are a series of plastic Superquinn shopping bags on the floor beside the fridge, full of food for tonight and ready-meals for the week ahead. The dishwasher is humming.

The children have evidently enjoyed the zoo much more than Fintan had thought, and they bombard Conor with a torrent of enthusiasm about it all: the chips, the piglets, the bongo, the owl, the lot. Conor is smiling as he listens, but Fintan can see behind his smile a deep melancholy; and as the other man looks at his daughter, Fintan sees again that wounded, all-consuming love that he had noticed earlier.

At the door when they are leaving, he again has to fight the urge to give the other man a hug. Conor shakes his hand hard, and claps him on the back.

'Thanks for looking after her and giving her such a good time.'

'Don't mention it.'

'Take it easy, Fintan.'

On the morning of the day that Fintan takes the children to the zoo, Beth and Martina are also engaged with animals, albeit of a more domestic kind. The cat has caught a mouse. Or rather, it is in the process of catching a mouse, and it is Beth, standing at the kitchen window, still in her dressing-gown, who notices it first. She points it out to Martina who is just about to leave for work.

The cat and mouse are sitting close together and neither of them moves. Then the mouse makes a sudden run and the cat is after it, stops it with her paw. She picks it up in her mouth and jumps up onto the windowsill. The effect is horrific and hilarious in equal measure, for the drooping body of the mouse makes for the cat a walrus moustache, so that it looks like an old gent in a Victorian photograph. Beth and Martina both shriek at the sudden closeness of the cat and the mouse, inches away on the other side of the pane of glass. The cat hops down again and releases the mouse, but it doesn't run. It rears up on its back legs, waving its paws in the air while the cat sits, immense, over it. She pretends to look away and still the mouse does not move. There is almost something complicit in it, the mouse hypnotised by fear, so that it seems to conspire in its own fate.

Martina grabs a brush from behind the door. 'I can't bear this,' she mutters, and goes outside. 'Shoo! Shoo! Bad cat! Leave the mouse alone!' The cat holds its ground as Martina waves the brush at her. The mouse runs a little distance and then stops again, as if it can't understand what's happening. The cat slinks off to get at it, defying Martina, who shouts at her again and goes after her with the brush. 'Stupid mouse,' she says, 'Run! Run!' and finally it does, slipping behind a dustbin and disappearing.

Martina is in bad form when she comes into the house, even though she has saved the mouse. Beth protests gently, saying that it's the cat's instinct, and that better she go hunting than that the place be overrun with mice.

'I know, I know,' Martina says, 'but it's the cruelty of it, the way she plays with them that I can't stand.' She kisses Beth goodbye and leaves for work. As soon as she has gone, Beth opens the back door and lets the cat into the house.

'Bad cat! Bold!' she says, but she doesn't really mean it. The cat stares up at her insolently. 'Poor little mouse.' With her tail high, the cat stalks off into the living room. Through the open door, Beth can see her settle down and start to wash herself, systematically and comprehensively.

Beth makes tea and sits at the kitchen table, drinking it, and thinking about Martina and how inordinately upset she seemed to be by what had happened in the yard, even though the mouse had escaped; even though Martina can't stand mice. After all these years together, there are still times Beth finds it hard to second-guess her. She's tender-hearted, but she's a complicated woman, too, Beth thinks. While she had never expected that they would end up living together, the pair of them—who could possibly have foreseen that?—nor had Beth ever thought that Martina would simply marry and have a family and be happy.

How could she have easily found love when she hadn't been loved by her own mother? It pains Beth to think this, but she knows it to be true. She remembers Martina as a small child, remembers her trying to solicit attention from Joan on many occasions and being rebuffed. Beth had found herself com-

pelled once to remonstrate with Joan about it when Martina
was about four. They'd been at the beach together and Martina
had come up, excited, pleading with her mother to come and
see the sandcastle she'd made, and Beth had been taken aback
at how coldly Joan had dismissed her. She'd watched the little
figure plod back down the damp sand towards the sea and,
meek as she was, Beth couldn't let it pass.

'It wouldn't hurt, just to go and look at it, and it would
mean a lot to the child.'

'If ever you were to have children of your own, you'd
understand that you can't be giving in to them at every end and
turn.' The barb found its mark. Without another word Beth
stood up and walked down the beach to where Martina was
standing, barefooted and forlorn, beside the great hump of her
sandcastle.

'Will we go and look in a pool? We'll lift the weed, and we
might find a crab or a shrimp.'

Was it any wonder that as she got older Martina had started
to play up, to be headstrong and petulant? What other way did
she have of making her mother pay attention to her?

Fintan of course had always been different, a softer, more
biddable child than Martina; and Joan had never seemed to
have it in for him to the same degree that she did for her
daughter. Beth remembers Joan saying around the time that he
went to university, 'Fintan has good functional intelligence.' It
was a phrase that struck Beth as both accurate and damning. It
admitted his good mind, but suggested a lack of originality and
imagination. The life he has now is the one that might have
been predicted for the nice, rather ordinary little boy she
remembers: the good steady job, the solid marriage, the children.

The cat is still washing itself, repeatedly licking its paw and
wiping it over its left ear, so vigorously that the ear is turned
inside out. Beth picks up her tea and carries it into the sitting

room, the better to observe the cat, and also to avail herself of the morning light, which is powerful. It affords the strange little room, and all the objects in it, a kind of grandeur. Beth settles herself on the sofa, and the cat continues washing its face.

The marriage that had produced Beth and Joan hadn't been the happiest, as the family would euphemistically put it, when they spoke of it at all. It had left Joan militant—*she* wouldn't be bullied or harassed by her husband, the way her own mother had been—and it had left Beth fearful of men; wary of relationships, let alone marriage. She found a job in an office, and after their parents were dead and the family house was sold, she rented a small apartment. If, as life went on and she entered middle age, it felt lonely to put her key in the door each evening and know that she was going into an empty flat, the consolation that at least she would not be walking in on an argument was an increasingly bleak one.

She'd been at a symphony concert in the National Concert Hall one night, on her own because she had no one with whom to go, and had found herself sitting beside a man, about her own age, with blue eyes and sandy hair. He'd asked if she would like to borrow his programme, not realising that she had one herself; and so they had fallen into conversation about the music they were to hear that night, and about the concert season, for which they both had subscriptions. He taught music in a secondary school, he told her, but it was more than just a job, music was his life. The concert began, and when they talked again in the interval they discovered that they both had tickets for another concert taking place in two weeks' time. He suggested that they meet beforehand; and so that second evening began with tea beneath the great crystal chandelier and concluded with drinks together in a hotel across the road from the concert hall, where they made plans to meet again.

Her new friend Christy, she discovered, had been the only

child of an exceptionally happy marriage. They had made a quaint little family, slightly odd, and Christy knew it, freely admitted as much: 'People used to call us "The Three Bears."' He was devoted to both his parents and had nursed them through their final illnesses. He had had a serious girlfriend, he told her when he knew her better, but with the pressure of his job and his sick parents something had to give, and it was the relationship that didn't make it. And so here he was now, alone in middle age, still living in the house which was not just where he had grown up, but his father before him.

'The House Time Forgot' was how he described it to her before he brought her there for the first time. 'It's a peculiar place, but you'd expect that in my home, now wouldn't you?' She'd realised that that was fair comment. He was sweet-natured, he was kindness itself, and that he was also slightly eccentric didn't bother her at all.

Beth had been well warned, then, about how strange the house would be, but she hadn't been prepared for its extraordinary appeal. Even as she remarked upon the old-fashioned details—the leather-bound books in the bookcase with their gold-stamped spines, the wooden obelisk of the metronome on top of the piano, the oval mirror with bevelled edges—she was more aware still of the atmosphere of the room. There was a sense of deep peace, as if the happiness of decades was annealed into the very air. All the love, all the contentment had lingered on. And it was not on that same day, but it was in that room that Christy was to ask her, in a circumspect way, to marry him: 'Do you think you would like to live here? With me? Forever?'

He'd insisted that they have a proper wedding: nothing too showy, that wouldn't have been their style, but not a hole-and-corner affair either. Beth bought a lilac suit, and there had been a string quartet in the church. A reception for twenty-five people was held in one of the best restaurants in Dublin, with champagne and an elegant white cake. They went to Venice for their honeymoon; and the morning after they returned a tiger kitten in a basket was delivered to Beth, a surprise wedding present from Christy and the first of the succession of cats that would share their life together in the following twenty years, concluding with the failed mouser lying at Beth's feet this morning, who has finished washing herself and is now fast asleep.

Christy had believed that everything happens for a reason. He said that when something bad happened, something good would always happen as a result; and that although the good thing would not justify or negate the bad it was important to recognise and value it. He would have been very happy to know that Beth is now living with Martina.

Beth can remember those last days very well too, because she has made a point of doing so. She has taken the time over the years, as she is doing now, to rehearse in her mind exactly what happened.

She dates it from the Sunday. She had gone up the street for an hour or so, to visit one of the neighbours, whose daughter had had a new baby. Beth had been invited to see it, so she'd left home with a small gift after lunch, and got back again at about four. Christy had all the dishes done and was sitting beside the fire he had promised to have lit by the time she got back. But he'd looked very serious and he asked her to sit down. She'd asked then if there was something wrong.

'Martina's here. She's upstairs sleeping.'

Beth can remember how astonished she had been, for Martina's visits home had always been long in the planning, the dates circulated months in advance. Never once had she turned up unannounced like this.

'Martina? But why? What's she doing here?'

'I don't know.'

'Did you ask?'

'Ah no, and please don't be asking her yourself either. She's upset about something. She'll tell us in her own good time if she wants. She's booked into some hotel out at the airport, but I'd rather she stayed here. Would you be all right with that?'

'By all means. But is she ill?'

'No, I wouldn't think so.'

But when Martina had come downstairs some time later looking shattered and wan, Beth wasn't convinced, for she had the air of someone getting out of bed for the first time in a week, after a bad bout of flu. There was something timid and quiet about her. Christy had behaved as if everything was perfectly normal, talking about the music on the radio, and saying that when she was ready he could take her out to the airport hotel to collect her things; pulling Beth into the conversation and saying that they were both delighted that she would be staying with them, and Beth agreeing.

While they were gone Beth had prepared a meal for the evening, salads and cold meats, but on their return Martina said that she wasn't hungry. She wanted to change into her night clothes, even though it was still quite early, and Christy said why not, told her to unpack and settle in. And so she went upstairs while they ate. When she came down again, in night-dress and dressing-gown, Christy brought her tea and toast in to where she sat by the fire. She smiled at him then, and Beth realised that it was the first time she had seen her smile since she had arrived.

'I might sleep late in the morning, if that's all right,' she said, and they both told her to do as exactly as she pleased.

Beth can't remember much of Martina's presence in the house in the following days, partly because she maintained a low profile, but primarily because, ever since, Beth has focused on her memories of Christy at that time to the exclusion of most everything else.

The day after Martina arrived was a Monday, and in the

118 - DEIRDRE MADDEN

afternoon Christy and Beth had gone to a garden centre to buy bedding plants: lobelia, violas, million bells. Christy had read the newspaper out in the garden after breakfast on the Tuesday, and then later in the day they'd planted up the flowerbeds. On Wednesday they'd had lunch out, soup and sandwiches in a cafe near home that Beth particularly liked. But she can remember some of the details from those days with preternatural clarity: the blue shirt he'd been wearing on the Monday; the pottery bowls in which the soup had been served; the way when she went to him in the garden with his paper he'd reached out and taken her hand, put it against his face and held it there for a moment, then kissed it before releasing her again with a smile.

And when she thinks about it now she can indeed remember Martina being there, almost as a ghostly presence to begin with, but becoming more apparent as time passed. She insisted on cleaning out the fire on the Tuesday; she helped Beth fold linen from the hot-press, and cooked dinner for them all on the Wednesday night. She told Christy, who in turn told Beth, that she had been in touch with the place where she worked to say that she wasn't well and wouldn't be in for the rest of that week, and was that all right?

'I told her I would ask you,' he said, 'but that as far as I was concerned, she could stay here for as long as she needed. She looked troubled and uncertain at the thought of going back.' Beth agreed with him that if Martina needed a haven at that time then it was good that they could provide one.

But the main thing she remembers about those days are the ordinary activities in which she and Christy were engaged, and which had formed the texture of their daily life throughout the years they were together: doing crosswords, sewing a button onto a jacket for him, making scones, the cat sleeping on the sofa, the radio playing, Christy reading a library book. On the Wednesday night he had gently brushed her hair away from her face before they got into bed and he kissed her; he had wished her sweet dreams, as he always did. And then he fell asleep, never to wake up again.

Afterwards, she would be glad that his life had had such a gentle ending, without pain or fear. Afterwards, she would realise that it was an extraordinary stroke of good fortune that Martina was staying with them, so that she, Beth, had help immediately to hand when it happened. Afterwards, she would be surprised at how easy the transition was when Martina moved in permanently with her, how right it seemed and how well it worked. But all of these realisations came long afterwards. At the time Beth's grief and shock had been such that she had thought she, too, might die.

All of that was more than ten years ago, and this is the reality of her life now: old age, Martina, and this house, where the morning sun warms the fur of the sleeping cat, and touches everything it falls upon with eternity.

THIRTEEN

Fintan is on his way to visit his mother, having put it off for as long as is conscionable. Joan is one of those people who drain energy from those around them. She does this to such a degree that sometimes, when he is with her, Fintan feels that he is caught up in a science fiction story, and that his mother is an alien masquerading as an elderly Dublin woman, who siphons off energy to convert it into—what? Inert gases? An alternative fuel? Some kind of antimatter? Fintan has no idea. All he knows is that he habitually leaves her company feeling so depleted that he thinks he might have to lie down on the pavement, outside the apartment block where she lives, until he has recovered. So unpleasant an experience is this that he avoids visiting her until the guilt provoked by staying away ('Maybe you've forgotten where I live?') begins to outweigh the misery of actually going there.

And so this Saturday afternoon finds him on the DART, that is, the suburban train that sweeps around Dublin Bay from Howth in the north to Glenageary in the south, where Joan lives, and beyond. There is at least the consolation of coming to the stop where he usually gets off to go to work, and staying in his seat as the train moves off again.

Joan will be expecting him. He phoned yesterday morning to see if a visit today would suit her, as Joan can't stand spontaneity in any form. He is bringing her gifts: a packet of smoked salmon from one of the several fish shops along the pier in Howth, and a large bouquet of sunflowers, both items having been purchased by Colette that morning. Fintan doesn't know why women love flowers so much. Colette had suggested that Rob send his girlfriend Mags a bouquet for her recent birthday, a gesture which triggered a flood of such rapture—'Nobody ever sent me flowers before! Nobody! There were roses! Twelve of them! Pink ones! I cried!'—that Rob had found it faintly alarming. (Niall to Rob: 'And to think that you might have given her a gift token.')

Fintan is deeply grateful to Colette for having bought the fish and the flowers. He thinks now of what his life would be without Colette, and has a sudden vision of himself walking around with no head, an image as compelling as it is ridiculous. He is still troubled by his encounter with Conor the previous week, although Colette herself has been briskly dismissive of his concern regarding Emma's parents, telling him that every marriage is a law unto itself, and that many break down for reasons incomprehensible to those outside them. Further, she remarked that every marriage ('And I mean *every* marriage, Fintan') carried within it the seeds of its own possible destruction, and that the failure to recognise or admit to this increased the risk. Colette can still surprise him, even after all these years and three children together. Sometimes he thinks that is what is wonderful about her. Sometimes it worries him.

Fintan's mother lives in an apartment block a short walk from the DART station. It is older than the one in which Conor lives, not as contemporary and stylish but with mature gardens around it, and a settled community in which Joan feels at home. She has been living here for many years now. With her husband dead, Martina gone and Fintan married she had sold the family home, an attractive old house also in Glenageary, and bought this place. It is one of a few things which Fintan feels Martina is unreasonable to hold against Joan: the family home was much too big for one person, and what Joan has now is more practical and easier to maintain, even though

Fintan himself secretly regrets the loss of the home in which he grew up, and avoids the road where it is. The thought of other people living in there unsettles him.

Joan comes right out to the front door of the building to let him in and to greet him. He kisses her and she exclaims with delight at the bouquet.

'Such flowers! They're like the sun itself! They'll light up the room for me.' They exchange pleasantries and small talk as he follows her down the hall to her ground-floor apartment, and he asks himself, as he sometimes does initially when they meet, why he had dreaded so much going to see her; for she seems—she is—a perfectly pleasant old lady, not the passive-aggressive, manipulative little head-wrecker he imagines when he is away from her, although he wonders how long it will be before the first signs of conflict appear. Almost immediately, the slow attrition begins.

'And you don't have Lucy with you?'

Fintan says no, that Colette has taken her to the hair-dresser's.

'Well that's a disappointment, I had been looking forward to seeing her.'

One–nil. As he sits down on the sofa he realises that he is still holding the paper bag with the fish in it, so he hands it to her.

'Smoked salmon. You couldn't have brought me anything more welcome.'

An equaliser in the second minute. She takes the packet of fish from the bag and waves it at him sternly.

'Now if you could get that son of yours to eat some of this, it would do him good. He can't be getting the protein he needs from those nuts or greens or whatever it is that he lives on.'

Two–one.

Niall, who is now in his first year at university, became a vegetarian around the time he learnt to read and write. What amazes Fintan about this is not Niall's fidelity to his regimen so much as the refusal of others to accept it, even after all these years. Moreover, Niall shows a patient acceptance of endless comments and questions that even Fintan can see are foolish and tiresome. If people gave Fintan as much grief about rump steak as they do Niall about mung beans, he would tell them where to get off. Niall attempts to convert no one to his cause, but will politely discuss the subject if asked to do so.

Even Mags had been on at Niall lately: 'But when you smell a rasher do you not just think you'd love one?' 'No.' And then he had spoken of what he called 'the politics of food.' Fintan had been overhearing this and listening idly, as Niall clearly and patiently explained how it took so much land and energy to produce food for farm animals and that, given how many people there were in the world to feed now, it was much more logical to simply eat plants, rather than feed plants to animals and then eat them. To his surprise, all of this made perfect, logical sense, even to Fintan, who would as soon eat his own shoes as renounce meat.

'You have to admit,' he says now, 'that Niall does look well on his vegetables.' The younger son is clearly the healthiest member of the family. He is slim, with sleek shiny hair and clear skin. While the rest of the Buckleys cough and snuffle their way through the winter, Niall rarely catches a cold or flu. But Joan will have none of it.

'A man needs to eat meat,' she insists. 'You'll be glad to know,' she continues, 'that there's good ham in those sandwiches, not rabbit food,' and she nods at a laden plate on the table. 'Baked ham.' Fintan is indeed cheered to know this. 'I'll go make the tea, and I'll put these flowers in water.' Refusing his offers of help, she goes off to the kitchen.

While he is waiting for his mother to come back, Fintan stands up and wanders around the room, inspects the family photographs that are on display. There is a large picture of Rob from his school days, in his rugby gear, and a much smaller one of Fintan and Niall in the back garden in Howth. There is a photograph in a silver frame of Colette, and another of Joan herself holding Lucy in her christening robe, a family heirloom. Someone—he can't remember who—had once told Fintan that displays of family photographs give you a more reliable sense of the real regard in which people are held than anything that might be professed, and, looking at the pictures, he thinks that this is fair comment. The room is comfortable without being cosy, and is furnished in neutral colours—beige, cream, and touches of chocolate brown. There are Lladró figurines, two small oil paintings of seascapes, and a standard lamp with a pleated shade. These are the only things in the room that Fintan remembers as also having been in his family home when he was a child.

Joan comes back, first with the sunflowers, which are a shock of sudden brightness in the room, and then returns with the teapot, which is under a padded cosy in the shape of a country cottage, complete with chimneys and embroidered window boxes. Fintan remarks upon it, says that it looks like something Beth might have, and Joan narrows her eyes as she pours the tea.

'Who do you think gave it to me? It's practical though, I have to admit that.' She settles back in her armchair with her cup and plate and she sighs. 'I don't know how Beth lives in that dark, dingy little house, truly I don't; and I don't know why she doesn't do something with it, now that she has a free foot. Take down those picture rails, and that wooden panelling in the hall. All those nasty woolly pictures; all that embroidered stuff: I'd get rid of it. Nice pot of magnolia paint would make a world of difference to that place. I'll never forget the first time I went there. I thought I was dreaming. I thought I'd made a mistake and ended up in some kind of folk museum, with houses from a hundred years ago. Olive-green walls. I ask you!'

'I think Beth has always really liked it,' Fintan protests weakly.

'If Christy liked it, Beth would like it. She'd have followed that man into the sea. And he didn't want to change a single thing his mummy had made or bought. A little mummy's boy, that's what he was.'

Joan has never quite recovered from the shock of Beth's marriage, of her sudden refusal to be the dowdy spinster, the maiden aunt no longer.

Sometimes when he is in meetings with Imelda at work, Fintan plays a little game with himself, scoring points for each phrase as it comes up: five for 'going forward,' 'challenges,' and 'thinking outside the box;' ten each for 'low-hanging fruit' and anything that 'washes its own face.' He plays a similar game with Joan. If she refers to Christy with her habitual phrase, Fintan will allow himself an extra cake.

'Getting married!' Joan says. 'I'll never forget it. Beth coming to me. "I've met a very nice man. I'm getting married." And her past fifty already. "Christy, his name is." A most insignificant man, that was what I thought when I met him.'

Involuntarily, Fintan's eyes flicker towards the plate of cakes. He chooses two, then turns to his mother to defend Beth's late husband. Not liking Christy, Fintan thinks, is like finding a dark side to St. Francis of Assisi. He has had this conversation with Joan many times before.

'I can't agree with you there, Mummy. I thought he was a wonderful man, so kind and gentle, the perfect match for Beth. He made her very happy in the years they had together. And as regards the house, it's not quite as fusty as all that. Even in Christy's day, they had a stereo, a little telly and so on. They did make some changes over the years, and there's been more done since Martina moved in.'

'Martina! She fell on her feet, didn't she? Coming back like that, once she'd got tired of London, as I knew she would someday, when the gallivanting was over. Martina was one of those girls who thought they'd be young forever.'

'I think it has all worked out for the best,' Fintan insists. 'Martina and Beth look after each other. They're very happy together.'

'Enough of that,' Joan says dismissively. 'Tell me this now, Fintan: how are you?'

She is sitting opposite him and she stares directly into his eyes as she asks this question. What does Joan see when she looks at her only son? Someone who is not quite a failure, but not quite a success either. Given who and what he is, together with what he has done and achieved in his life, one can only wonder at the criteria which she is applying. But Fintan is aware of her judgement, as of yore, and wilts under it.

'I'm good,' he says, unconvincingly.

'And that wonderful wife of yours?' There is no irony in this question. Although Joan thinks he could have done better—much better—on the employment front, and perhaps have raised a second son less weedy than Niall, she has no reservations about his choice of a wife. Over the years she has grown to be very fond indeed of Colette. This is a testament in itself to Colette's extraordinary qualities—although even she had failed to make a good initial impression on her future mother-in-law, the first words Joan had ever spoken to her when Fintan impulsively brought her to Joan's door on a rainy day having been: 'Wipe your feet.'

Fintan reports that Colette is well, and Joan asks after Rob, another favourite, in whom she sees Fintan's own considerable intellect, uncompromised by a soft heart. She admires Rob for his steely personality, and predicts a prosperous future for him. Each of the Buckleys, Fintan thinks as he talks now to his mother, is either a hawk or a dove. Rob is a hawk, Joan too. There is even something hawkish about Martina, which is possibly one of the reasons why she doesn't get on with Joan: there are more similarities between them than either would wish to admit. Fintan's father had been a dove, Niall is one, and Beth, too, of course.

After work last night he had gone to meet an old friend for a drink. The man concerned had texted to say he would be twenty minutes late, which didn't unduly bother Fintan, waiting on a banquette with his pint of Guinness. Sitting nearby he noticed a young woman dressed, like his colleague Imelda, for the corporate world in a navy trouser-suit and a pale-blue blouse with the collar out over the jacket. She was in her early twenties and pretty; but there was a hardness about her eyes, the set of her mouth, so that the prettiness was undermined by something unattractive in her personality, as Colette's plain features were redeemed by her kindness. On the table before the woman was a packet of cigarettes, a lighter and a glass of white wine. She was frowning at a mobile phone in her hand, jabbing at it, texting. Looking at her, she seemed to him vaguely familiar, but at first he couldn't place her. Perhaps she had temped with his company? He didn't think so. She had a snub nose and a high forehead. The phone she was holding rang and she answered it. 'I saw him, yeah. Last night. Yeah, I know, but I don't care. "Lucy," he said to me, and I said, "Don't you 'Lucy' me. If you think I'm letting you away with what you did last Saturday you can go and . . ."'

And at that, Fintan realised with a shock who he was seeing.

A hawk, then, he thinks now with sorrow. Lucy will be a hawk. He has long since accepted that there are aspects to his sons' lives and personalities that he doesn't know about, and with which he has no desire to engage. But he still finds it hard to think of the adult into which Lucy will grow.

He has more tea and a cake, but when he moves to take his second cake, his prize, Joan challenges him on both his diet and his health, charges with which Fintan is familiar, and which he wearily refutes.

'I'm quite well, really Mummy, there's no need to be concerned.'

But his mother insists, and they argue about it until he ends up vaguely promising to go for a full medical check, something which he has no intention whatsoever of doing. To distract her, he changes the subject to the economy, and the ploy works. Somewhat to his surprise, he begins to find himself genuinely engaged in the conversation, for her ideas on the subject are original and well informed; her gloomy predictions worryingly convincing.

At the end of the afternoon, when he stands up to leave, Joan suddenly says, 'I know it was very hard for Beth, losing Christy when she did, but it was hard for me, too, and no-one ever seems to think of that. I was left with two teenagers when your father died, and Martina was a complete handful. It wasn't easy for me either.' There is petulance in the words, but none, surprisingly, in the tone of voice, which is perhaps why Fintan feels that what she is saying is only the truth and that she is right: she was never given the sympathy she deserved. She looks vulnerable, standing there in her living room; her age and weakness strike him as never before.

'It must have been very hard, Mummy,' he says. 'I didn't appreciate it at the time; I was so young myself.'

Afterwards, when he leaves the house and is back out on the path, he has to fight the urge to lie down for a while, before going down to the station and getting the DART back to where he lives. In the train, the people around him look strange; he feels edgy and enervated.

When he arrives in Howth, instead of going straight home he walks down to the pier to clear his head. The water between the boats is oily and dark green, with the texture of glass in a bathroom window, rippled to make it opaque. Below the surface a dark shape is thickening, looming, and the head of a seal breaks the surface, whiskered and oddly humorous. Written in bold red letters on a white sign nearby are the words: 'A person shall not feed a seal from the quayside or from any other place in this port,' with further details in small print of the bylaw to which this pertains. Fintan wishes he had a pocket full of herring. The seal looks up at him, as if this might well be the case. For a few moments they stare at each other, the seal in all its heavy innocence, until it finally slips below the surface of the dark water again, and disappears.

FOURTEEN

M artina can't sleep, and so she rises, puts on her dressing gown and comes downstairs. She considers herbal tea, but only for a moment, and then pours herself a good inch of single malt, a thing she rarely does. Maybe it'll help me sleep, she thinks. Maybe it'll just make me drunk. No matter.

Her gaze wanders around the room as she sips the whiskey. She has lit only a small lamp, and all the strange objects there look stranger than ever: the vase with the suspended glass lustres; the old gramophone with its golden horn; the embroidered fire-screen. She imagines Christy's mother sitting decades ago in that same room, with a piece of buff linen stretched taut on a wooden hoop and small hanks of coloured silk beside her, each one bound with two black-and-gold paper bands. Christy's father is sitting behind a big newspaper. Christy is upstairs asleep: he is still a baby. All of this is a fantasy and yet it is also the truth: all of this really happened. It is odd to think of this space holding the lives of these three other people, only one of whom she ever met. Martina sometimes comes home from work, enters the hallway and is astonished to think that she is living in this peculiar little house.

There are framed photographs here and there: Fintan with his entire family; Martina and Beth; a picture of Christy on his own that Beth particularly liked, and that Martina had had enlarged and framed as a Christmas gift.

Martina remembers that when she lived in London she had

gone through a phase of visiting flea markets and junk-shops, where once she had seen for sale a photograph of a woman in late middle age. It was a studio portrait, black and white, and probably from the early nineteen-fifties, Martina guessed, from the clothes the woman was wearing. She couldn't imagine that anyone would ever wish to buy it. The image was in no way striking or special but it was moreover enormous, quite out of proportion for a family photograph. And Martina had found it an easy image to interpret: this was a matriarch, and this photo was a devotional object, at which the family was to worship. It worked for a while, didn't it, Ma? She thought. But you ended up in the junk-shop, all the same.

Martina sips her whiskey and wonders idly about the woman in the photo. Is she remembered with dislike by her family? Or is she remembered at all? That will be me someday, she thinks, completely forgotten, like my sultry ancestor, about whom nobody remembers anything, not even her name. Martina thinks about her own life: all the things she has done, all the things that have happened to her. Things that had been so important at the time: possessions she had wanted, the attention of certain men; why, she can almost laugh at it now, so trivial and foolish do her past desires seem to her. Everything will be forgotten, everything.

She is sitting at a kitchen table with a box of thick wax crayons and a cheap jotter. She is drawing pictures. Granny Buckley is baking scones. She has the wing of a white bird to clean the griddle and she is singing. Martina draws flowers, a rabbit, a clumsy house. The rain is battering down outside. There is no sign of Fintan or Edward.

She can feel the effect of the whiskey now, not just the slight burning sensation that she had registered with the first drink and its following glow, but the way it is working on her mind too, she finds that dangerously attractive. It isn't just the wish to take the edge off the day, but to wipe out the accumulated pain of life itself. She knows it would solve nothing, but on a night like tonight she can understand the appeal of the mental annihilation strong drink might bring.

There is a room in her mind. The door is shut, but sometimes it blows open and she is drawn in against her will, on a black wind that leaves her shaken and frightened. Sometimes she can enter the room of her own volition, to try to face down what is there. Might she be able to go there tonight?

She met him at a party hosted by a friend of a friend. He'd been part of a small group which she'd drifted up to and joined; four or five people there had been, two of whom she knew casually. They'd been talking about gambling. It was something in which she had no interest, but she'd stayed there listening anyway for a few moments, until another person had come over, at which point the group suddenly split, leaving her with him and a woman whom she didn't know, who said to him, 'Well, Duncan, how was New York?'

It turned out that he had lived in Manhattan until recently, which interested Martina as she had been there for a visit some six months earlier. It was only really at that point in the evening that she paid him any attention at all. He was about the same age as herself, a professional type, dark-haired and heavily built, formally dressed unlike most of the other guests. She said that although she had liked being in New York for a week, she had wondered how it must be to live there, and so they had talked about that, and about places in the city they had particularly liked. The other woman took part in the conversation for a while and then moved away.

At that moment platters of food were brought around, and someone came up to them with two bottles of wine, to top up their glasses. There was a balcony in the apartment where the party was being held and it was a warm night so he suggested that they sit out there to continue the conversation.

He was in IT, he told her, like pretty well everyone these

days, she thought, and afterwards she wondered if what he said was true, was anything true, was his name even Duncan? She wondered if she were to go to the friend of the friend and try to trace him back, would anyone claim him?

Out there on the balcony, with small candles flickering in lanterns suspended from the railing, Martina realised that the more she talked to him the less she liked him. Nor did he seem particularly taken with her; he struck her as offhand and indifferent. And that had irked her. She was used to men paying her court, but she was also aware that she was getting older. Of late she had become particularly sensitive to any idea that the power of her beauty might be waning. Before long she stood up to leave, and was surprised when he at once asked if they might meet again.

She said yes, but made it clear that it was to be on her terms. She suggested the following Saturday, and gave him the name of a wine bar near where she worked, said she would see him there. He was amenable to all of this, but still seemed neutral, as though it would have been a matter of no consequence to him had she refused.

Why did she agree to see him again? She was, in the future, to ask herself this time without number. Perversely, it was because she had known he didn't like her. It was a challenge. She would win him over; she would make him attracted to her. But in all of this she was refusing to listen to her instincts which, even then, told her that he wasn't to be trusted.

To Martina's surprise, he seemed delighted to see her the following Saturday, jumping out of his seat to greet her when she arrived. She found him much more engaging than he had been at the party: funny and charming, keen to know all about her. He wanted to know where she worked, and where she lived in London. She enjoyed the evening, and when he suggested dinner the following Saturday night, she readily agreed. He knew of a particularly good restaurant, he said; fish, it served, did she like fish? He would book a table there for eight o'clock. It was a bit tucked away and hard to find, so he would collect her from her apartment and drive her over. She also agreed to this.

She isn't sipping the whiskey any longer, she is gulping it down. She rises, goes to the bottle and pours herself some more. As she returns to her seat she notices that the cat has chosen not to sleep on Beth's bed tonight, but is on a chair, in a dim corner of the room. Martina picks the cat up and it gives a soft, petulant mew; but when she sits down and places it on her lap it flops over and immediately falls asleep again. She strokes its fur as she drinks. This is another thing she has learnt during her time living with Beth: the deep solace an animal can give, its mute comfort. She puts her hand on the cat's breast and can feel its rapid, racing heart, its life-force giving her strength.

He arrived early, a good three-quarters of an hour before she was expecting him, so that she was still in her dressing-gown, which annoyed her. He kissed her hard on the mouth as soon as she opened the door, which annoyed her even more, and he pushed quickly past her, was in her living room before she knew what was happening.

'I'm nowhere near ready.'

'I can wait.'

It was all wrong. She felt vulnerable and wrong-footed, and his personality was different again tonight on this third meeting, there was a swagger, an arrogance that hadn't been there before. He stood in the middle of the floor looking around freely at everything in her modest home: it seemed to amuse him.

'Maybe this isn't such a good idea. I think we should call dinner off.'

'You're very unfriendly all of a sudden.' He crossed to where she was standing and touched her face, but roughly, and she flicked her head away, showing her anger frankly now.

'Just go.'

With that, he hit her hard across the face with the flat of his hand, using such force that he knocked her to the ground. Then he was on top of her, pinning her down, pulling her dressing-gown open. She screamed once and he hit her again, put his hands tightly around her throat and told her to stop struggling. What happened was pure violence. She went very silent and still, like an animal, like prey, because she was afraid she was going to die.

Afterwards as she lay there, crying and in deep shock, he laughed at her and told her she was a stupid bitch, asked her if she'd enjoyed it, said it would do her good. He left the room and she heard the main door of the apartment close behind him.

Fear. Fear such as she had never known. He might come back. Although she was in great pain she struggled to her feet, went into the hall, double-locked herself in and put on the chain, then went back and dragged the sofa up against the living-room door.

I got it all wrong, she thinks now. I should have called the police. I should have got them to take swabs, try to trace him back through the people at the party. I should have nailed him and stopped him attacking some other woman. Martina feels guilty about that, and guilty and ashamed too that she hadn't seen him for what he was. She hadn't been some *ingénue*, some little girl just out of school. She'd prided herself on her judgement as far as men were concerned: years of experience had taught her not just how to subtly read all kinds of strategies and behaviour but how to deal with it. Even with this man she had known that there was something wrong; but out of vanity, she told herself, she had ignored the danger signs. In fairness, though, she'd never before come across a dangerous predator. She'd thought that he didn't much like her; but could never have guessed at the degree to which he hated and despised her, until it was too late.

And she is angry with herself now, sitting half-drunk in the dim room with the sleeping cat, for feeling any degree of shame or guilt, knows that this poisonous combination of self-blame and recrimination is the natural result of what had been done to her. It wasn't her fault.

After locking herself in that night, she took a shower, and put the dressing-gown she had been wearing in a bin bag to be disposed of. She was still terrified that he might come back. He didn't just know where she lived; he had asked her most specifically where she worked.

It didn't take long to dress and to pack a case, even though she was unsure what to put in it because she didn't know where she was going. She was struggling now against confusion and disorientation, struggling to stay focused. She took the Tube out to the airport even though it was not the quickest means, but the thought of being closed up in a taxi with a man she didn't know was intolerable to her.

In Heathrow she looked up at the destination board and thought of how she could go, this very night, to any of the cities listed, the more distant and unfamiliar the better. There was a flight going out near midnight to Tokyo: she could max out her credit card on a one-way ticket and spend the time during the journey trying to work out what she would do when she got there. A flight was also leaving shortly for Oslo. When Martina had first moved to London she had had a Norwegian neighbour, a funny, gentle, friendly woman. Maybe all Norwegians were like that. Maybe she should go there. What should she do?

Just with that, she flinched away in shock as someone touched her gently on the arm.

A middle-aged woman was standing beside her in jeans and an anorak, pulling a small suitcase on wheels. She asked Martina in an American accent was she well, did she need any assistance? And Martina discovered that she was too traumatised to speak. The stranger then said, 'I'm going over there,' and indicated a nearby cafe. Martina shook her head helplessly. 'I'll be there for the next half-hour or so. If you change your mind and need anything, come and find me.'

A few moments later, Martina looked at her own reflection in a mirror in the ladies and could see why the woman had approached her, offering help. Would she herself have gone up to someone who looked as she did? Someone so tousled and with a look of such terror in their eyes? She splashed water in her face and brushed her hair; told herself to get a grip or she would put herself in danger again. These thoughts of flying to Japan, it was madness, but still she wanted to get away; still the thought of being in the same city, the same country, even, as that man, appalled her.

She went out onto the concourse and looked at the destination board again. The last flight of the day to Dublin was listed. If she bought a ticket and checked in immediately she would just about make it.

What she remembers most clearly from the rest of that night was the huge surge of relief as the plane took off, and the sense that this was the right thing to do, even if it was also somehow mad and unreal and nightmarish, like all of the rest of that evening. I was at work today, she thought. A few hours ago I was selling skirts and dresses and jackets, and now I'm on a plane. She felt a mixture of fear and adrenaline that sat particularly badly with her physical exhaustion and distress, and did not improve as time passed.

What next? The cool, damp Dublin air when the door of the plane was opened. Wheeling her case to an airport hotel no distance from the terminal and booking in. The anonymous room. Putting out the 'Do Not Disturb' sign, and pulling a table across the door, just to be sure. Another shower, with cheap liquid soap from the pump bottle in the bathroom. The sleep that didn't come until near dawn.

She puts her face down close now to the cat's head, breathes in the pleasant, peculiar fragrance of its coat. It's doing her no good to remember all this. Think about the next day, the Sunday. Ringing Fintan around noon and being secretly relieved when it went straight to voicemail. Not being able to venture out until the afternoon, and then taking a bus into town, with no real idea of where she was headed, any more than when she had gone to the airport in London; but getting out of the bus in Drumcondra and walking towards Christy and Beth's house, as if under a spell.

I'm safe now. That had been her first thought when Christy opened the door and she stepped into the hallway. That man would never find her here, no more than if she had somehow slipped through a rent in the fabric of time itself, and disappeared back into the distant past. Christy said almost nothing—maybe he didn't even speak at all. In the sitting room he gestured towards an armchair before a newly lit fire. For once, there was no music playing in the house. There was a Foxford rug on the back of the sofa in Black Watch tartan, blue, green and black, and he handed it to her. She unfolded it and sat under it, stroked the wool with her hands and felt oddly consoled. She thinks that she then moved to speak but he raised his hand, and they sat in silence for a few moments longer: but such a silence. It deepened and intensified. Any word would have been too abstract to define what had entered the room, but the spirit of it was the absolute antithesis of what had been done to her the night before.

She picks up the sleeping cat and settles it again on the chair where it had been earlier, the same chair where she had sat on that afternoon. It was bizarre, she thinks. Christy had been dead by the end of that week. All their lives had been in turmoil; Beth had been inconsolable. Martina's own grief for what had happened to her merged with the shock of Christy's passing; she had been able to conceal it from the family. In time

Beth had started to piece her life together again; and part of that had been Martina's decision to give up her job and apartment and relocate to Ireland. There was no point in thinking *what if?* That was what had happened, and this is the reality of her life now.

The clock on the mantelpiece strikes three. Martina has to go to work in the morning. She places the empty glass beside the clock and goes upstairs, hoping for sleep.

FIFTEEN

'Who's that?'

'I don't know.' Imelda has caught him out. Fintan minimises the image on his computer screen, but she'll have none of it.

'Pull that up again; let me see it.' He does so, reluctantly, and they both look at the photograph that appears. It shows a woman in a blue dress of the style of the early twentieth century, standing by a white gate.

'She's not in costume,' Fintan says. 'It's a real colour photograph, from a hundred years ago.'

'Amazing,' Imelda says, bending over the computer and staring at the picture. 'I didn't know you were interested in photography.'

'I am a bit, yes,' he says, trying to sound offhand.

To his relief she straightens up and moves away. She's wearing a grey trouser-suit today, with a cream blouse. She surprises him then by saying, 'If my house was on fire, the first thing I would grab would be a photograph. Well, I mean after I'd grabbed the Jack Russell, of course.'

'Not the kids?' Fintan is aware that Imelda has two daughters, who are roughly the same age as his own sons.

'The girls are big now. They've got legs. They know where the front door is,' she says ironically.

'And the Jack Russell doesn't?'

Imelda laughs. 'If the house did go up in flames, it would probably be the dog that made sure we knew about it. The least I could do in return would be to carry the little mutt to safety.'

'And the photograph?'

'Oh it's nothing special,' she says, becoming evasive. 'Just a snap, you know? But it means a lot to me. It's a family thing.' Fintan says nothing: not as a tactic, but because he can think of nothing to say. Imelda feels compelled to speak into the silence, adds hesitantly, 'It's just a picture of a birthday party from when the children were small. The four of us. There's a cake on the table, all the little candles, and there's a balloon tied to the back of a chair. We all look so happy. It's like everything my family means to me is in that photograph.'

'A picture like that would be very precious,' Fintan says, to help her out, aware that she's becoming uncomfortable. 'I sometimes think photographs had more value when they weren't so commonplace; when they took more effort. We're drowning in images nowadays. All the phones with cameras on them; people must take more photos than they ever look at. I sometimes wonder what the point of it is.'

Imelda smiles at him. 'You're getting old, Fintan.'

'That's what my kids say to me.'

'Mine too. The unfortunate thing is that it's true.'

She remembers then the reason that brought her in to see Fintan in the first place: she wants to collect some documents relating to an important meeting which is to take place the following day. She says she'll read over the papers and come back soon to discuss them with him; and with that she leaves the room. He should get back to work again once she's gone, but he doesn't. He stares at the woman in the blue dress and thinks about everything that has happened to him in recent weeks. The hallucinations and strange shifts of perception are still occurring, but they are becoming less frequent, and he is getting rather used to them. He is sensible these days to an immense pathos in life, and finds himself fervently hoping this awareness will never again leave him.

Yesterday had been a day of particularly fine weather. In the evening when he was going home, everything had been bathed in a golden light with a tinge of pink to it, against which the grey stones of certain buildings and the bell tower of a church he passed stood out with an enhanced monumentality. He had found himself thinking, first: The sky today is an eighteenth-century sky, and then, immediately: Why am I thinking this? What do I mean? He teased it out in his mind on the DART as he went home. The sky had reminded him of how it looked in old prints of Dublin with which he was familiar, eighteenth-century prints where the main focus was on the architecture. This in turn made him think of what Niall had said to him some weeks ago, of not confusing the medium used to suggest a thing with the thing itself. And yet the sky he saw was the thing itself: this was how it looked today, but it was also how it would have looked on certain days in the eighteenth century. It pointed up again his tendency to think of the past as profoundly different to the present, which it was, but not in the ways he expected; so that he had been surprised by Rob's remark of a week ago on a cold day of torrential rain, when Fintan had found him in the hall gloomily sluicing water off his leather jacket and flapping his black umbrella: 'They would have had weather like this during the Famine. Do you ever think about that, Dad? Rain like this and rotten potatoes.'

There's a knock at the door. Imelda has returned, having read the documents. Fintan comes out from behind his desk and they both sit down to discuss the meeting the following day. He's paying attention and is fully engaged to begin with, but the shift, when it comes, is irresistible and relentless.

He finds himself watching the scene from a distance, as if he is an observer rather than a participant in what is happening. This has happened to him before, but never so completely.

It doesn't stop. It's as if he's sliding away not just from himself and from Imelda for a moment, but from his entire world, and forever. Now he feels that he is looking at the scene from another dimension, from a point beyond time itself. He realises that he is dead. So is Imelda. So are Colette, the children, his entire family, everyone he knows, the people he had seen on the DART this morning: everyone, indeed every creature now alive in the world, is dead. The civilisation, for want of a better word, in which he lives is over. This is how it is for the Babylonians, for the people of Ancient Greece. How had he thought he would ever escape? And he had thought that, he realises now, albeit in a most inchoate and confused way. Perhaps the strangest thing of all is that this sudden knowledge does not perturb him. Instead of being grief-stricken he feels a kind of cosmic gratitude: the life that he has been given!

The grief comes when he realises that the sequence is now in reverse. He is going back through time and again it is relentless, so powerful that it feels as if he is also moving through space. The scene in the room—tiny, as if viewed through the wrong end of a telescope—of two people sitting in an office, papers in their hands, is getting bigger and bigger, so that he can see it in more detail all the time, until he is no longer looking at the scene, but is in it. He is sitting there looking at the documents before him, and Imelda is making exactly the point she was focused upon when he slipped away to experience immortality.

He hasn't missed a thing.

SIXTEEN

Fintan is in bed with the lights out, and Colette is already asleep beside him. He is wearing pyjamas so hopelessly uncool, such classic passion-killers that his sons, when they see him wearing them, or observe them pinned on the clothes-line, wonder mutely how it was that they themselves ever managed to come into being.

Fintan is thinking about the strangeness of sleep, of the body's need to sink below consciousness for around eight hours of each twenty-four that pass; a need so profound and imperative that there are special rooms and furniture in every home, special clothes devoted to this state. It is, Fintan thinks, wholly at odds with the functional, rational nature of contemporary life. A great many people are in denial about the need for sleep, and make it a point of honour to get by on five or six hours, perhaps even less. He thinks of how exhausted Imelda often seems to him, and how annoyed she is if he comments upon this, even sympathetically; as though being tired were some kind of moral failing, some kind of vice. Everyone wants to have more time: time to work, to make money; time in which to be active and do things. There's a general consensus in the modern world that the days are too short to fit in every-thing that needs to be done; and, given this, it seems counter-intuitive, perverse, even, to spend eight whole hours lying in the dark, sleeping and dreaming. The earth conspires with the body, sending the darkness of night to gently encourage and facilitate sleep.

Tomorrow he will go north with Martina. When he had rung his sister after dinner to finalise plans for their journey, she had said something that struck him as strange: 'This isn't about the past. You do understand? It's very important.'

'I know that,' Fintan had replied. But it wasn't true. He'd had no idea what Martina had been talking about; for what is the whole point of this trip, he thinks now, if not to find a way back into the past, into their childhood, to a lost world only half-remembered, but *real*? They are to meet again with Edward, who had been a part of it, and who can share in those memories as no one else in the family can, either because they hadn't been there, or because they hadn't been born at the time. That is what delights Fintan about the prospect of tomorrow. That, surely, is the point of it, even though he had agreed with Martina that it wasn't. He's excited about the visit, but also slightly apprehensive.

Eventually he drifts off. No one in the family is having any trouble sleeping tonight: Fintan and Colette, Rob, Niall and Lucy, Martina, Beth, and Joan.

Some three months have passed since first we met Fintan, sitting gloomily in a restaurant, eating chocolate almonds. In the course of that time much consideration has been given to the past, and so we should, perhaps, give some thought to the future.

What is going to happen in Ireland at the end of the first decade of the twenty-first century has been so exhaustively reported upon elsewhere as to not need significant comment here: suffice it to say that the years of prosperity through which people have been living is followed now by a spectacular economic crash. It is perhaps interesting to note, in light of Fintan's recent thoughts, that one of the first in a series of dramatic events, as everything begins to unravel, will take place in the middle of the night, namely the bank guarantee.

All the citizens of Ireland will be asleep. Government ministers will have to be woken from their beds to go and take part in this historic event. The people of Ireland, including Fintan and Colette, will wake one morning some two years hence and, turning on their radios, will be stunned to discover that during the night the heads of all the major banks have gone to the government and obliged it to honour all of the banks' considerable debts. People will think they must be imagining things; that they must be still asleep and dreaming, but no: it is a fact. It will soon become apparent that the banks were mendacious in their dealings with the government on that night, and that their debts are far greater than was then admitted to. Things get worse and worse, leading a couple of years later, at the end of the decade, to the intervention of the external agencies and the loss of economic sovereignty. This would be traumatic for any democracy, but is felt particularly keenly in Ireland, given its history.

The fallout from these events will affect every family in the country, including the Buckleys. Although a great many of his co-workers, including Imelda, will be made redundant, Fintan will be spared. Rob, however, on graduating from university will be unable to find work, and will be one of the many people, both young and old, who will be obliged to go abroad. He will go to Australia, and will find a job with an insurance company in Sydney. Mags's mother, whose health is poor, will be unable to face letting Mags, an only child, follow Rob. For a while they will try to maintain the relationship over the great distance that separates them; but a year after Rob's departure for Australia they will decide, by mutual consent and with great sadness in the entire family circle, to go their separate ways in life.

Apart from Rob and Mags themselves no-one is more upset about this than Colette. Her intuition that they were well matched was perfectly correct; and had circumstances been different they most certainly would have stayed together and formed a partnership as enduring, stable and harmonious as that of Fintan and Colette; would have produced in due course a few bright toffee-haired, gap-toothed children, for both sets of grandparents to dote upon.

Niall will finish his degree and then do an M.Phil. in art history in Dublin, followed by a Ph.D. in London. Fintan will at times wonder if his younger son will be studying for the rest of his life: the idea of Niall with a job becomes worryingly unimaginable to him. Although he has longed to see the back of his sons, he will find that he misses them terribly, once they are gone. He will particularly miss Rob, whom, as is the case with all his children, he loves dearly, even though he had frequently found him to be a smart-alecky little know-all, a view not incompatible with love. The idea of Rob being on the other side of the world will make Fintan vertiginous with loneliness for him. He will not confide in Colette about this, as he will not want to add to her own sadness about Rob's absence.

Martina will have endless struggles to keep her shop open in the harsh new economic climate. She will share her worries with Fintan, who has a sharp business mind and a good head for figures, and who will give her valuable advice, so that she comes through in the end, and is not forced to close her doors as she will so often fear.

And so the Buckleys will certainly have their problems in the future, but they will have much luck and happiness too. All of them will enjoy good health, in itself a great gift. Rob will return from Australia in his early thirties; he will find work, a partner, produce children. Niall, in spite of Fintan's misgivings, will not just find a job, but will have an outstanding career as an art historian, working at various art institutes and universities in Europe and the States, before settling in London where he will be appointed to a Chair. He will also have a happy marriage and a family. The love and affection that is already there between Martina and Colette will deepen and strengthen. The passage of time will blunt the worst of the rough edge in the relationship between Joan and Martina. Death, when it comes for Joan, will be sudden and clean. Beth will drift towards the end in a slow, gentle decline, aware of what is happening to her, but peaceful because she feels sure that afterwards she will be reunited with the spirit of Christy.

Of the three Buckley children, it is Lucy who will struggle most. It will be a shock to her to discover that the love of a man is not always unconditional, profound, and disinterested. No-one will ever love her as much as her father. It will be hard for her to come to terms with this, and her emotional life will become a restless quest for something she will never find. The fate of Emma will be quite different. After an increasingly truculent and disruptive adolescence, during which even Colette will become uneasy with the idea of her as a friend for Lucy, Emma, in her early twenties, will meet someone whose family background is equally fractured and dysfunctional. They will have two children and set up home together, get married and have two more, creating for themselves a refuge from the past. Their home will be for them a haven, albeit a noisy and crowded one. They will be together for the rest of their lives; they will live to see their children's children.

But how can all of this be known, when it has not yet come to pass? We all of us look towards a personal future that is imaginary; although the absence of either tragedy or remarkable good luck may indeed deliver up to us, as though we were somewhat inept fortune-tellers, a rough approximation of what we think is going to happen. To engage too much with the future, in all its fragility and uncertainty, can make us feel dizzy with unease. Let us think, then, of the past, so that we may speak of real things that have actually happened; conscious always that the past, like the future, also shimmers behind the veil of imagination.

Let us think about the Buckley's beautiful ancestor, whose

studio portrait is in their possession, and to whom Martina bears a strong resemblance. Her name, although the Buckleys will never know this, was Agnes O'Donovan. She was born in Dublin on the fourth of December, 1886, and at the age of eighteen she married a greengrocer in Rathmines, called Patsy McGrath. The following year she gave birth to a daughter, whom she named Grace. She died in childbirth with her fifth baby on the twenty-fourth of April, 1916, which was Easter Monday, and therefore, by extraordinary coincidence, the very day of the Rising. Agnes remained as a luminous memory in the mind of Grace, who was eleven at the time of her mother's passing.

In due course Grace made what turned out to be an unhappy marriage with a man called Felim Ryan. They had two daughters, Joan and Elizabeth, known as Beth. The loss of Agnes was so great a sorrow to Grace that she never spoke of it to her children; and with Grace's own passing in the early nineteen-sixties, Agnes slipped from memory to oblivion. But the effect of her being on those around her was incalculably diffusive; and fact alone gives an inadequate sense of that being: of her kindness, her wit, her magisterial beauty. Let me show her to you.

Here she is kneeling in a city church, before a bank of small, white candles with fluttering flames. She is conventionally religious in the manner of the day. Her head is bowed in prayer.

Here she is in the photographic studio, bewitching the poor photographer: amused at his shy confusion, smiling at him flirtatiously, so that he is relieved to retreat under the privacy of his camera's black cloth, from where he stares frankly at her hazel eyes, her red-gold hair, and wishes he could take her photograph in colour.

Here she is working in her husband's shop in a long white apron, holding court amongst the cabbages and carrots; looking out for the lonely and making people laugh.

And here she is, sitting alone on a bentwood chair before a marble-topped table in a cafe, staring blankly at the piece of cake before her. She is warming her hands on a little white teapot, and she is thinking about the future, wondering what it holds for her.

Let us leave her there and return to the present: to her great-grandson Fintan Buckley, asleep with his wife Colette beside him, and all of his children still under his roof. Tonight, as so often, all of Ireland lies under a soft thick blanket of cloud. The wind rises, and soon it begins to rain.

But none of them hears it: only the cat, awake and alert, sitting in total darkness at the top of the stairs in Beth and Martina's house; only the cat lifts its head and listens to the sound of the raindrops. And if either woman, in the drowsiness of sleep, were to suddenly switch on the light and come upon it there on the landing, the cat, with its folded paws and perfect markings, might well appear to them fabulous as a unicorn.

SEVENTEEN

I t's the following morning. The rain has stopped, at least for now, and Fintan and Martina are sitting in her car outside his house. Already their plans have been disrupted, by Fintan having left the lights of his own car on overnight and drained the battery. Martina has driven over to collect him, rather than his collecting her, as had been the original plan. He has climbed into her car only moments earlier and has been somewhat overwhelmed by the force of her physical presence in such a confined space: her perfume, her abundant hair, her silk scarf printed with tulips. She is staring straight ahead through the windscreen, lost in thought, and then she turns to him.

'We'd best get going.'

Later, as they move onto the motorway, Fintan cannot help wondering if his flat battery was something of a Freudian forget, an unconsciously deliberate mistake. He dislikes driving and is only too happy to let Martina take the wheel, although he had felt when planning the trip that he should offer to take them north. And so things are working out well. It's rare for him to have a good block of time on his own with Martina. Usually he meets her in the company of Beth, or over at his own house with all of his family. He has noticed many times before now that she will always relax and talk in the car; and as the road slips past they update each other on their lives in recent times. They talk about her job, about his, about Joan and Beth, about Colette and the children. Already Fintan is enjoying the day.

Not long after they pay the road toll and head for the border Martina says, 'I never told anybody this, but I was afraid back then, up in the North. I thought we might get shot or blown up. I didn't like seeing the soldiers about the place. But I liked being with Edward and Granny. I enjoyed the animals and the countryside, so I didn't let on that I was scared. Joan stopped us going anyway. Are you nervous about seeing Edward again, after all these years?'

He hasn't realised that he was until Martina asks him this question. 'Maybe just a bit. I have this image in my mind of a little boy and of course he's a grown man now.'

Edward had given Martina directions on the phone as to how to find the house, which she had written down and which Fintan now reads aloud as they approach Armagh. Their cousin is still living in the old home-place, the house where they had stayed as children, and Fintan now realises that he is also anxious about this, as well as about seeing Edward again and meeting his wife Veronica. He feels slightly melancholy to realise that he needs directions, that without them he would be unable to find his way back.

They turn off the main road onto smaller, narrower byways, which are flanked by rolling green hills, hedges, and trees. There are cattle grazing on the bright grassy slopes; and already something is beginning to wake in Fintan's memory. He does not recognise any given house, field, or hill, but the generality of them speak to him. They are all familiar in a visceral way, and he knows deep down that he has been here, or hereabouts, before now.

Suddenly Martina stops the car abruptly. 'There's something I want to look at here.' She puts the car in reverse and they go backwards along the road for about a hundred yards, to an old ruined farmhouse, which Fintan hadn't noticed as they passed it. To the side of the house is a grassy lane which Martina overshoots, then she changes gear and drives into it.

'This will only take a minute,' she says, switching off the engine, 'and we have plenty of time.'

They get out of the car and Fintan sees that behind the house there is a farmyard with stables. He realises exactly where he is, even as Martina says, 'This is the place.'

The air is moist and fresh after the stuffy car. They walk tentatively into the yard and stand there, looking around. It's a long time since any horse has poked its head out of these stables. All the doors have been padlocked shut, but to what purpose? Most of the padlocks are rusted, and in one case the top part of the half-door has rotted away and swung open, so that it gives onto a square of perfect black space. Fintan turns to Martina, who is standing in the middle of the stable yard, looking thoughtful.

'How did you know this was here?'

'I recognised the gable at the side of the house; that is, as we were driving past, I thought there was something familiar about it. I didn't realise that this was where the photograph was taken, but I felt that there must be some connection, and that I'd like to have a closer look. I didn't expect this. I'm as surprised as you are.'

Whatever Fintan had thought he might feel were he ever to come back to this place, he isn't feeling it. He isn't feeling anything.

'At least you now know what the colour is,' Martina remarks, but he doesn't know what she means.

'The doors,' she says with a touch of impatience, pointing at them. 'When we looked at the photograph, you wondered what colour the doors were.'

The stable doors are dark green. The paint is chipped and worn, and the whitewash of the stable walls is scuffed and grubby. The cobbles of the yard are broken and uneven; briars and ugly weeds shoot up from the juncture between the walls and the ground. It is so strange to see Martina standing there.

She looks as if she is taking part in a fashion shoot in a deliberately incongruous place: an abattoir, a town dump, a neglected stable yard. The place somehow defamiliarises her to Fintan.

He walks over to the open half-door and peers into the darkness. He can see nothing, but he suspects that there may well be nothing to see. There is the dank smell of old things: rotting wood, rotting vegetation. Suddenly he is startled by a little bird flying out; it swoops and is gone.

'What do you think?' he asks his sister.

'I'm astonished that this place exists. I mean, that it still exists. It was just somewhere in a photograph. I never thought that we might find it; that we would ever be here again.'

'Me neither.'

'I wasn't even looking for it.' They stand in silence for a moment or two longer, and then Martina looks up at the sky. 'It's going to rain,' she says. 'Let's go.'

* * *

There's some debate when they arrive at Edward and Veronica's house as to whether or not it's the right place. Fintan insists that it can't be. It's a two-storey building, like the home-place, but it looks quite new and has dormer windows, with stained-glass panels on either side of the front door. Martina agrees, but says that she followed Edward's directions exactly, and that Fintan must admit the surroundings are familiar, which he does. With that, the front door opens and a man waves to them where they're still sitting in the car.

'Fintan?' he calls. 'Martina?' Martina gives a little cry of delight as she recognises Edward, and she hurries to him. He embraces and kisses her; he gives Fintan a half-hug and a bone-crushing handshake. He's wearing brown corduroy trousers, with a petrol-blue pullover and an open-necked check shirt.

His face is like something in a dream, Fintan thinks: perfectly familiar and yet translated into something different from what he remembers. He's a middle-aged man with a tanned face, freckles, and sandy hair. Weirdly, when he smiles, something of the look of Rob shimmers in his eyes.

'Isn't this great?' he says, as he ushers them into the house. 'We should never have left it so long.' Edward's wife Veronica emerges from the kitchen, a country woman, kindly and smiling. She is introduced to Fintan and Martina, and leads them all into the sitting room, where a fire is lit in the grate. They hand over the gifts they have brought with them: a good bottle of whiskey, an orchid in a pot, and a box of chocolates. They're rather anodyne presents, Fintan thinks: trying to decide what to give had made him aware that he no longer really knew his cousin, and didn't know his wife at all; but everything is received with genuine delight and gratitude. Fintan feels oddly shy and at a loss, unlike Martina, who is clearly happy and relaxed, and for whose company he is deeply grateful.

'So what's the story with the house?' she asks, as they settle in, and Edwards laughs.

'We have everyone bamboozled over that.' He explains that some four years ago they had needed to put on a new roof, but in the course of preparations for the work had discovered a host of other problems, including advanced dry rot. 'It had never been the most practical place—it was hard to heat and some of the rooms were very poky, as you'll well remember. We thought about it and decided that the place needed so much work that we might as well knock it down and start from scratch, get a decent modern house. So that's what we did.'

Martina compliments them on it and Fintan murmurs his assent; but in truth he regrets the loss of the old home-place, its dark rooms, its flagstones and deep windows. The new house seems to him to lack character. The sitting-room walls are painted a buttermilk colour. There are chintzy curtains, a vase of silk flowers sits on a nest of pine tables; and all of this occupies the exact place where the home-place once stood. As Martina, Veronica, and Edward talk about double-glazing and damp-courses, Fintan imagines another house contained within the shell of this one: a dream-house, eternal, where the three of them are still children and Granny Buckley is still alive and always will be.

Martina tells them that she lives with her aunt in an old house and she describes it to them, its quaint strangeness, and how it came to be like that; tells them vaguely about how she came to be living there.

'And what about you, Fintan,' Edwards asks, turning to him. 'How are your family? They must be well up by now. Are any of them married and away?'

'I wish,' Fintan says fervently, and they all laugh. He talks to them about his family, about Colette, Niall, Rob, and Lucy. He regrets that he didn't think to bring photographs with him, so that all he has is a couple of rather limited snaps that he keeps in his wallet. He tells them about the children's lives, their studies and their plans, such as they are. Veronica and Edward talk about their daughter, who is married and lives nearby, and their son, who is at college in Belfast.

'And how's your mammy? Is she well?'

Fintan says that Joan is fine, but he cannot in any sincerity pass on good wishes, not least because neither he nor Martina have told Joan about this trip to the North.

'I never knew your mammy well,' Edward says. 'She never came up much to these parts, did she? It was always your daddy who drove you up when you were coming to stay.'

They fill each other in on the detail of their lives, and bring each other up to date. Edward has worked as a motor mechanic for most of his adult life, and has his own garage a few miles down the road. The family has got out of farming completely. The few fields the Buckleys had weren't enough to make a living from these days, and the land, which they still own, is set to a local man in an adjoining farm. Veronica works part-time as a teacher in nursery school. Martina tells them about her life in London, and about the shop.

As they talk, Fintan remembers something Colette had once told him. When they announced their engagement, Joan, unexpectedly, and in a gesture somewhat out of character, had hosted a celebratory lunch for them, inviting Christy, Beth and Martina, the latter attending with good grace for Fintan's sake. Colette had told him about looking at these people sitting around the table, none of whom she knew well at all at that point, and realising that they would be in her life forever afterwards, and she in theirs. What Fintan feels today is something similar. There's that strange combination of distance and intimacy. Already he feels connected to Veronica, who had been a stranger until he met her less than an hour ago. Even Edward he would have passed in the street without recognising him: indeed, it's possible that he has already done so, for Veronica has mentioned that they both like Dublin and go there from time to time, for GAA matches and for shopping. There's a forty-year hiatus in their knowledge of each other, and yet still he feels profoundly close to Edward, feels that he knows him in a way that he doesn't know Imelda, with whom he spends the best part of each working day, and has done so for many years.

In due course, they are taken into the kitchen for tea. Fintan and Edward sit beside each other at the table, with their backs to the window, and the two women sit opposite. Veronica has prepared for them a classic spread, with ham and salad sandwiches. She has made fruit scones, and there's jam, both raspberry and blackcurrant, served in small glass dishes. There are chocolate biscuits, and an apple tart with fresh cream. She brings a metal teapot from the hob and pours tea into fragile cups sprigged with roses, offers them sugar and milk. It reminds Fintan of the old days, and leads to them talking about Granny Buckley: there's much laughter as they swap anecdotes.

When they have finished their tea and stand up, Martina nods to Fintan, indicating that he look behind him. There, through the kitchen window, is the old orchard of the home-place, looking exactly as he remembered it, as if at any moment soldiers might materialise out of the trees, moving towards the house.

They go back in to the fire and Martina says, 'Don't forget to show Edward the photograph.' From a large envelope he has brought with him Fintan takes the picture of the farmyard with the stables. He passes it to Edward, who laughs with delight, and calls Veronica to his side.

'This was taken at the farm just up the road,' Edward says.

'I know,' Martina replies. 'We happened on it by chance when we were on the way here.'

'I must call by to look at it myself, some of these days,' Edward says softly. He is still staring at the photograph, and he laughs again, but Fintan can see that he is deeply moved.

'You have it all clear in your mind,' he says, lifting his head and looking directly at Fintan, 'and then you see a thing like this and it all seems like a hundred years ago.'

They stay for more than another hour; and by the time Fintan and Martina are ready to leave they all feel that solid bonds of friendship and family have been established amongst them, bonds they are keen to maintain.

'Don't make it so long until you come again,' Veronica says. Fintan promises that he will bring Colette and Lucy with him the next time; Veronica and Edward say they will arrange for their children also to be there. They say that they will let Fintan and Martina know when next they're in Dublin. Their cousins embrace them and wave them off from the step; Martina toots the horn of the car in farewell.

EIGHTEEN

W here does it all end? Perhaps here, in a country pub, somewhere between Armagh and Dublin. It seems as good a place as any to conclude. After the visit, neither Fintan nor Martina is in a rush to get back to the city. Both are keen to have a little time to decompress, to process the day's events, and so they have sought out a hostelry; got lucky, too, for it's a good one, snug and appealing, with low beams and an antique mirror advertising soda water, another one advertising Guinness. They've installed themselves in a corner beside the fire. Fintan has ordered a large Bushmills and is getting quietly, happily, sozzled. He rarely drinks spirits and so they go straight to his head when he does; and he's also very careful with his behaviour concerning alcohol when his children are around, wanting neither to give them a bad example, nor to spook and upset them. This is noble of him, as he loves strong drink, so that a glass of whiskey or a cognac is a great treat, and one in which he rarely indulges. He's aware of Martina watching him from the other side of the table, faintly amused, but he knows that she understands completely where he's at with this, and why he needs it. Martina is drinking black coffee.

He's aware, too, that each of them is in a very different mood, although he isn't quite sure why. Meeting Edward has left him euphoric. He feels a kind of elemental delight that reminds him of the births of his children. He knows that he has been babbling on excitedly ever since they left the house, long before he started drinking. Martina, however, has been unusually pensive and quiet.

'You were absolutely right about one thing,' he says. 'It wasn't about the past.' Martina puts her head to one side and looks at him curiously.

'What makes you say that?'

'Because it wasn't. It just wasn't. If you think about it, we spent far more time talking about our lives as they are now, rather than talking about Granny Buckley and when we were children.'

'That's true,' Martina concedes.

'When we were in the stable yard, it was so strange. I recognised it, more than remembering it. But I'd thought I'd feel differently if I were ever to be there again, in the place where that photograph was taken. I mean, I thought I'd feel *something*. And I didn't. Nothing at all.'

'Neither did I. But I seem to have drawn a different conclusion from the day to you. It did make me think about the past rather than the present, and about how completely over it is: you can't really get at it again.'

'And it can't get at you either,' Fintan says, and again Martina looks at him quizzically.

'What do you mean?'

Fintan's at something of a loss as to know how to reply.

Martina turns and looks away towards the soda-water mirror, with its images of bottles and flowers. She blinks and presses the tip of her index finger to her lower lashes, blinks again, and suddenly Fintan sees her beauty figured forth once more: not just her physical beauty, but the light of her soul. She pulls the tulip scarf from around her neck and it flows down onto her lap, gathers there to form a luminous silken puddle.

'Do you want another drink?' she asks, turning back to him. Fintan shakes his head. 'Yes you do,' she says with a ghost of a smile. 'Don't tell fibs.' She gestures to the barman and points to her brother's glass. They sit in silence until the whiskey has been served.

'I hope you don't regret coming up here,' he says at last, and she looks surprised.

'No, not in the least. It's been a good day. Important. We'll come back again.'

The barman crosses to the fire and adds coal to it from a brass scuttle, momentarily quenching the flames, but they flare up again as the fuel settles. He engages them briefly in conversation about the weather, and Fintan asks him about the pub.

'You're not from around these parts?' the barman says, and Fintan and Martina smile at each other.

'We are, I suppose, yes,' Fintan replies, 'in a manner of speaking.' The barman lets it go at that.

When he has gone back behind the counter Martina says, 'I must see Colette one of these days for lunch. Will you tell her that?'

'She'll be more than happy. She always likes spending time with you.'

'She's a wonderful person.'

'She is. But so are you,' Fintan says, and Martina laughs.

'You're drunk, mister.'

'I may well be. But I'm happy. Very, very happy.'

Martina laughs again, pulls the coloured scarf from her lap and drapes it around her neck. 'Time, please, gentlemen,' she says. 'Ding! Ding! Drink up, please! Come on, mister,' as Fintan knocks back the last of his whiskey and stumbles to his feet. 'Time, please! We'd best be getting you home.'

Acknowledgments

I wish to thank John McHugh and the committee of the Heinrich Böll Cottage, Achill Island. Thanks also to Derek Johns and Linda Shaughnessy at United Agents; to Stephen Page, Hannah Griffiths, Mary Morris, and Rebecca Pearson at Faber and Faber; and to Paul Durcan, Mary and Angela Madden, and to my husband, Harry Clifton.

(alphabetical by author)

Fiction

Carmine Abate
Between Two Seas • 978-1-933372-40-2 • Territories: World
The Homecoming Party • 978-1-933372-83-9 • Territories: World

Milena Agus
From the Land of the Moon • 978-1-60945-001-4 • Ebook • Territories: World (excl. ANZ)

Salwa Al Neimi
The Proof of the Honey • 978-1-933372-68-6 • Ebook • Territories: World (excl UK)

Simonetta Agnello Hornby
The Nun • 978-1-60945-062-5 • Territories: World

Daniel Arsand
Lovers • 978-1-60945-071-7 • Ebook • Territories: World

Jenn Ashworth
A Kind of Intimacy • 978-1-933372-86-0 • Territories: US & Can

Beryl Bainbridge
The Girl in the Polka Dot Dress • 978-1-60945-056-4 • Ebook • Territories: US

Muriel Barbery
The Elegance of the Hedgehog • 978-1-933372-60-0 • Ebook • Territories: World (excl. UK & EU)
Gourmet Rhapsody • 978-1-933372-95-2 • Ebook • Territories: World (excl. UK & EU)

Stefano Benni
Margherita Dolce Vita • 978-1-933372-20-4 • Territories: World
Timeskipper • 978-1-933372-44-0 • Territories: World

Romano Bilenchi
The Chill • 978-1-933372-90-7 • Territories: World

Kazimierz Brandys
Rondo • 978-1-60945-004-5 • Territories: World

Alina Bronsky
Broken Glass Park • 978-1-933372-96-9 • Ebook • Territories: World
The Hottest Dishes of the Tartar Cuisine • 978-1-60945-006-9 • Ebook •
Territories: World

Jesse Browner
Everything Happens Today • 978-1-60945-051-9 • Ebook • Territories:
World (excl. UK & EU)

Francisco Coloane
Tierra del Fuego • 978-1-933372-63-1 • Ebook • Territories: World

Rebecca Connell
The Art of Losing • 978-1-933372-78-5 • Territories: US

Laurence Cossé
A Novel Bookstore • 978-1-933372-82-2 • Ebook • Territories: World
An Accident in August • 978-1-60945-049-6 • Territories: World (excl. UK)

Diego De Silva
I Hadn't Understood • 978-1-60945-065-6 • Territories: World

Shashi Deshpande
The Dark Holds No Terrors • 978-1-933372-67-9 • Territories: US

Steve Erickson
Zeroville • 978-1-933372-39-6 • Territories: US & Can
These Dreams of You • 978-1-60945-063-2 • Territories: US & Can

Elena Ferrante
The Days of Abandonment • 978-1-933372-00-6 • Ebook • Territories: World
Troubling Love • 978-1-933372-16-7 • Territories: World
The Lost Daughter • 978-1-933372-42-6 • Territories: World

Linda Ferri
Cecilia • 978-1-933372-87-7 • Territories: World

Damon Galgut
In a Strange Room • 978-1-60945-011-3 • Ebook • Territories: USA

Santiago Gamboa
Necropolis • 978-1-60945-073-1 • Ebook • Territories: World

Jane Gardam
Old Filth • 978-1-933372-13-6 • Ebook • Territories: US
The Queen of the Tambourine • 978-1-933372-36-5 • Ebook • Territories: US
The People on Privilege Hill • 978-1-933372-56-3 • Ebook • Territories: US
The Man in the Wooden Hat • 978-1-933372-89-1 • Ebook • Territories: US
God on the Rocks • 978-1-933372-76-1 • Ebook • Territories: US
Crusoe's Daughter • 978-1-60945-069-4 • Ebook • Territories: US

Anna Gavalda
French Leave • 978-1-60945-005-2 • Ebook • Territories: US & Can

Seth Greenland
The Angry Buddhist • 978-1-60945-068-7 • Ebook • Territories: World

Katharina Hacker
The Have-Nots • 978-1-933372-41-9 • Territories: World (excl. India)

Patrick Hamilton
Hangover Square • 978-1-933372-06-8 • Territories: US & Can

James Hamilton-Paterson
Cooking with Fernet Branca • 978-1-933372-01-3 • Territories: US
Amazing Disgrace • 978-1-933372-19-8 • Territories: US
Rancid Pansies • 978-1-933372-62-4 • Territories: USA

Alfred Hayes
The Girl on the Via Flaminia • 978-1-933372-24-2 • Ebook •
Territories: World

Jean-Claude Izzo
The Lost Sailors • 978-1-933372-35-8 • Territories: World
A Sun for the Dying • 978-1-933372-59-4 • Territories: World

Gail Jones
Sorry • 978-1-933372-55-6 • Territories: US & Can

Ioanna Karystiani
The Jasmine Isle • 978-1-933372-10-5 • Territories: World
Swell • 978-1-933372-98-3 • Territories: World

Peter Kocan
Fresh Fields • 978-1-933372-29-7 • Territories: US, EU & Can
The Treatment and the Cure • 978-1-933372-45-7 • Territories: US, EU & Can

Helmut Krausser
Eros • 978-1-933372-58-7 • Territories: World

Amara Lakhous
Clash of Civilizations Over an Elevator in Piazza Vittorio •
978-1-933372-61-7 • Ebook • Territories: World
Divorce Islamic Style • 978-1-60945-066-3 • Ebook • Territories: World

Lia Levi
The Jewish Husband • 978-1-933372-93-8 • Territories: World

Valerio Massimo Manfredi
The Ides of March • 978-1-933372-99-0 • Territories: US

Leïla Marouane
The Sexual Life of an Islamist in Paris • 978-1-933372-85-3 •
Territories: World

Lorenzo Mediano
The Frost on His Shoulders • 978-1-60945-072-4 • Ebook •
Territories: World

Sélim Nassib
I Loved You for Your Voice • 978-1-933372-07-5 • Territories: World
The Palestinian Lover • 978-1-933372-23-5 • Territories: World

Amélie Nothomb
Tokyo Fiancée • 978-1-933372-64-8 • Territories: US & Can
Hygiene and the Assassin • 978-1-933372-77-8 • Ebook • Territories: US & Can

Valeria Parrella
For Grace Received • 978-1-933372-94-5 • Territories: World

Alessandro Piperno
The Worst Intentions • 978-1-933372-33-4 • Territories: World
Persecution • 978-1-60945-074-8 • Ebook • Territories: World

Lorcan Roche
The Companion • 978-1-933372-84-6 • Territories: World

Boualem Sansal
The German Mujahid • 978-1-933372-92-1 • Ebook • Territories: US & Can

Eric-Emmanuel Schmitt
The Most Beautiful Book in the World • 978-1-933372-74-7 • Ebook •
Territories: World
The Woman with the Bouquet • 978-1-933372-81-5 • Ebook • Territories:
US & Can

Angelika Schrobsdorff
You Are Not Like Other Mothers • 978-1-60945-075-5 • Ebook •
Territories: World

Audrey Schulman
Three Weeks in December • 978-1-60945-064-9 • Ebook • Territories: US
& Can

James Scudamore
Heliopolis • 978-1-933372-73-0 • Ebook • Territories: US

Luis Sepúlveda
The Shadow of What We Were • 978-1-60945-002-1 • Ebook • Territories:
World

Paolo Sorrentino
Everybody's Right • 978-1-60945-052-6 • Ebook • Territories: US & Can

Domenico Starnone
First Execution • 978-1-933372-66-2 • Territories: World

Henry Sutton
Get Me out of Here • 978-1-60945-007-6 • Ebook • Territories: US & Can

Chad Taylor
Departure Lounge • 978-1-933372-09-9 • Territories: US, EU & Can

www.europaeditions.com

Roma Tearne
Mosquito • 978-1-933372-57-0 • Territories: US & Can
Bone China • 978-1-933372-75-4 • Territories: US

André Carl van der Merwe
Moffie • 978-1-60945-050-2 • Ebook • Territories: World
(excl. S. Africa)

Fay Weldon
Chalcot Crescent • 978-1-933372-79-2 • Territories: US

Anne Wiazemsky
My Berlin Child • 978-1-60945-003-8 • Territories: US & Can

Jonathan Yardley
Second Reading • 978-1-60945-008-3 • Ebook • Territories: US & Can

Edwin M. Yoder Jr.
Lions at Lamb House • 978-1-933372-34-1 • Territories: World

Michele Zackheim
Broken Colors • 978-1-933372-37-2 • Territories: World

Alice Zeniter
Take This Man • 978-1-60945-053-3 • Territories: World

Tonga Books

Ian Holding
Of Beasts and Beings • 978-1-60945-054-0 • Ebook • Territories: US & Can

Sara Levine
Treasure Island!!! • 978-0-14043-768-3 • Ebook • Territories: World

Alexander Maksik
You Deserve Nothing • 978-1-60945-048-9 • Ebook • Territories: US, Can & EU (excl. UK)

Thad Ziolkowski
Wichita • 978-1-60945-070-0 • Ebook • Territories: World

Crime/Noir

Massimo Carlotto
The Goodbye Kiss • 978-1-933372-05-1 • Ebook • Territories: World
Death's Dark Abyss • 978-1-933372-18-1 • Ebook • Territories: World
The Fugitive • 978-1-933372-25-9 • Ebook • Territories: World
Bandit Love • 978-1-933372-80-8 • Ebook • Territories: World
Poisonville • 978-1-933372-91-4 • Ebook • Territories: World

Giancarlo De Cataldo
The Father and the Foreigner • 978-1-933372-72-3 • Territories: World

Caryl Férey
Zulu • 978-1-933372-88-4 • Ebook • Territories: World (excl. UK & EU)
Utu • 978-1-60945-055-7 • Ebook • Territories: World (excl. UK & EU)

Alicia Giménez-Bartlett
Dog Day • 978-1-933372-14-3 • Territories: US & Can
Prime Time Suspect • 978-1-933372-31-0 • Territories: US & Can
Death Rites • 978-1-933372-54-9 • Territories: US & Can

Jean-Claude Izzo
Total Chaos • 978-1-933372-04-4 • Territories: US & Can
Chourmo • 978-1-933372-17-4 • Territories: US & Can
Solea • 978-1-933372-30-3 • Territories: US & Can

Matthew F. Jones
Boot Tracks • 978-1-933372-11-2 • Territories: US & Can

Gene Kerrigan
The Midnight Choir • 978-1-933372-26-6 • Territories: US & Can
Little Criminals • 978-1-933372-43-3 • Territories: US & Can

Carlo Lucarelli
Carte Blanche • 978-1-933372-15-0 • Territories: World
The Damned Season • 978-1-933372-27-3 • Territories: World
Via delle Oche • 978-1-933372-53-2 • Territories: World

Edna Mazya
Love Burns • 978-1-933372-08-2 • Territories: World (excl. ANZ)

Yishai Sarid
Limassol • 978-1-60945-000-7 • Ebook • Territories: World (excl. UK,
AUS & India)

Joel Stone
The Jerusalem File • 978-1-933372-65-5 • Ebook • Territories: World

Benjamin Tammuz
Minotaur • 978-1-933372-02-0 • Ebook • Territories: World

Non-fiction

Alberto Angela
A Day in the Life of Ancient Rome • 978-1-933372-71-6 • Territories:
World • History

www.europaeditions.com

Helmut Dubiel
Deep In the Brain: Living with Parkinson's Disease • 978-1-933372-70-9 •
Ebook • Territories: World • Medicine/Memoir

James Hamilton-Paterson
Seven-Tenths: The Sea and Its Thresholds • 978-1-933372-69-3 • Territories:
USA • Nature/Essays

Daniele Mastrogiacomo
Days of Fear • 978-1-933372-97-6 • Ebook • Territories: World • Current
affairs/Memoir/Afghanistan/Journalism

Valery Panyushkin
Twelve Who Don't Agree • 978-1-60945-010-6 • Ebook • Territories:
World • Current affairs/Memoir/Russia/Journalism

Christa Wolf
One Day a Year: 1960-2000 • 978-1-933372-22-8 • Territories: World •
Memoir/History/20th Century

Children's Illustrated Fiction

Altan
Here Comes Timpa • 978-1-933372-28-0 • Territories: World (excl. Italy)
Timpa Goes to the Sea • 978-1-933372-32-7 • Territories: World (excl. Italy)
Fairy Tale Timpa • 978-1-933372-38-9 • Territories: World (excl. Italy)

Wolf Erlbruch
The Big Question • 978-1-933372-03-7 • Territories: US & Can
The Miracle of the Bears • 978-1-933372-21-1 • Territories: US & Can
(with **Gioconda Belli**) *The Butterfly Workshop* • 978-1-933372-12-9 •
Territories: US & Can

31901067380693